H·I·T·C·H·H·I·K·I·N·G

·

Twelve German Tales

·

Gabriele Eckart

(Per Anhalter: Geschichten und Erlebnisse aus der DDR)

·

Translated & with an afterword & notes by Wayne Kvam

·

University of Nebraska Press · Lincoln and London · 1992

© 1992 by the University of Nebraska Press
All rights reserved. Manufactured in the United States of
America. Originally published as *Per Anhalter:
Geschichten und Erlebnisse*, © 1982 Buchverlag
Der Morgen, Berlin

Library of Congress Cataloging in Publication Data
Eckart, Gabriele. [Per Anhalter. English]
Hitchhiking : twelve German tales / by Gabriele Eckart;
translated and with an afterword and notes by Wayne Kvam.
p. cm. (European women writers series)
Translation of: Per Anhalter. Includes bibliographical
references. ISBN 0-8032-1814-1
ISBN 0-8032-6722-3 (pbk.) I. Title. II. Series.
PI2665.C52A8313 1992 833'.914–dc20
91-20299 CIP

Working on construction I had some truly existential experiences.
I got to know my own physical staying power. The construction site
was also important for me in that I found another language there.

Gabriele Eckart, interview in *Sonntag*, 1978

C · O · N · T · E · N · T · S

Translator's Acknowledgments   viii

Gabriele Eckart: A Profile   ix

The Woodlouse   1

The Tall Girl   8

Old Woman   25

The Attic   31

Construction Site: A Documentary   39

Philemon and Baucis   74

Feldberg and Back   80

A Week in Berlin   94

Street Sweepers   104

In Saubersdorf, beyond Glauchau   115

Uncle Benno   119

Hitchhiking   127

Translator's Afterword   135

Selected Bibliography   143

Translator's Acknowledgments

On different occasions I have
received the generous help of
Ursula Cedzick, Walter Grün-
zweig, Birgit Kirchhöfer, Lisa
Martinez, Madhu Mitra, Beate
Rodewald, & Gregory Shreve.
I remain grateful to Eugene
Wenninger and the Kent State
Graduate Research Council for
their support of literary trans-
lations. Finally I should like to
thank Gabriele Eckart, who
consistently provided me with
answers when I needed them.

Gabriele Eckart: A Profile

.

Gabriele Eckart was born in 1954 in Falkenstein, East Germany, in the mountainous region of Vogtland near the Czechoslovakian border. After attending primary and secondary school in the city of Auerbach, she entered Humboldt University in East Berlin in 1972. With a major in philosophy and aesthetics, she completed her *Staatsexamen* (M.A. level) in 1976. During the early 1970s, Eckart's poetry began to appear in East German newspapers and magazines; her chapbook *Poesiealbum 80* (Poetry Album 80) was published in 1974. Her first major collection of poems, *Tagebuch* (Diary), appeared in 1979, the same year that she became a member of the East German Writers' Union.

Early in her writing career Gabriele Eckart won praise for the youthful exhuberance and vitality expressed in her poetry. She also won the backing of Free German Youth, the massive organization for young people in the GDR supported by the Communist party. The more Eckart's reputation grew, however, the more uncertain her political outlook, the more wary her poetic voice became. A marked shift in her career occurred in 1978, when she held two blue-collar jobs, first as a cement worker in a construction plant and then as a street sweeper in downtown East Berlin. To give artistic expression to experiences such as these, Eckart turned from poetry to prose. The result was a collection of journalistic fiction, literary portraits, sketches, and short stories published under the title *Per Anhalter: Geschichten und Erlebnisse* (Hitchhiking: Stories and Experiences) in 1982.

In 1980, Eckart joined an agricultural cooperative in Werder (near Berlin) and used the opportunity to conduct individual interviews with a cross section of her fellow workers. Intending to publish the interviews in a collection entitled "Mein Werder-Buch/19 Tonbandprotokolle" (My Werder-Book/19 Tape-recorded Interviews), she met the resistance of East German censors. Ultimately the interviews were banned before their delayed publication date in 1984. Against the wishes of GDR authorities, Eckart turned to a West German publisher, Kiepenheuer & Witsch, and shortly thereafter her Werder interviews, *So sehe ick die Sache: Protokolle aus der DDR* (That's How I See It: Recorded Interviews from the GDR), became a bestseller in West Germany.

Subjected to increased harassment by the East German secret police, Eckart applied for a permanent exit visa in 1984, withdrawing her application only after receiving assurance that she could continue to publish in the GDR. Her second major collection of poetry, *Sturzacker* (Plowed Field), appeared in 1985, followed by the novella *Seidelstein* (Seidel Stone) in 1986. During the same year, *Per Anhalter* (Hitchhiking) was published in the West. By this time Eckart was clearly part of the opposition to the Honecker government, for she had aligned herself with the grass-roots peace movement that originated in the GDR's Evangelical churches and spread throughout the country.

An equally significant development came in 1986 with Eckart's opportunity, at age thirty-two, to travel to West Berlin and West Germany for the first time. "After you have sniffed a little bit of the world, you never want to lose the scent," she observed in West Germany's news magazine *Der Spiegel*.[1] The following year, Eckart was offered a guest lectureship at Denison University in Ohio and was permitted to travel to the United States. *Wie mag ich alles, was beginnt* (Liking Everything That Begins), her first

1. "'Ich kam mir überflüssig vor': Gabriele Eckart über einen Besuch in der Bundesrepublik," *Der Spiegel*, 3 March 1987, p.58. The translation is mine.

volume of poems to be published in the West, appeared at this time. In November of 1987, two years before the collapse of the Berlin Wall, Eckart chose to defect from her home country and to take up residence in the United States. In 1988 she was a visiting writer at the University of Texas in Austin. Currently she is associated with the German Department at the University of Minnesota. She resides in Minneapolis.

W.K.

The Woodlouse

·

So, the Woodlouse. One of the hundred old ladies collecting bottles and junk? Yes, judging from her coat, this most frayed of coats, mole-colored. These well-worn boots so big that I ask myself how many pairs of socks she could have on inside them. Her fur cap with only one earflap, secured under her chin with a piece of twine. And also this gesture, the way she pulls a glass out of the garbage barrel, meaningfully, almost devoutly, then rubs it with something like a cloth and sets it on the rickety cart with its wheels slanting outward.

But her look is different. Not so tired, so gloomy, discouraged, dull. Not full of sneakiness, slyness. Not someone who comes up and pounces on you. But when she turns around to glance at you . . . well, how exactly? The glance is somehow peculiar, as if it didn't belong to her.

But to find out these things I needed a few weeks. *Here*. In this quarter.[1] Where the walls are mangy as an old street dog and so squeezed together there's no end to the gloom in the streets and courtyards. The children are still pale after the hottest of summers.

This quarter, where they say the rent is collected with a revolver.

1. A reference to the borough of Prenzlauer Berg in East Berlin. An old working-class quarter with many apartment buildings in a state of neglect, Prenzlauer Berg became a haven for young East German writers, artists, and political dissidents during the 1970s and 1980s.

Where a city touring bus never risks getting lost. It's here that I live and grow accustomed to the Woodlouse, as she's called.

Pattering in front of me when I go grocery shopping, the cart behind her. The small, wiry figure with the lively step. The dignity of an important person.

Her daily greeting in this fresh, raw-throated voice. Her quiet omnipresence.

Even when she's not there. In the cellar, for example, next to her apartment house that is just as dark and damp. She spends her half a day in the cellar with the belongings she has passionately collected. These she arranges, sorts, dusts, polishes, and guards like precious objects: shopping bags made of string, brushes, plastic balls, small pieces of thread, ribbons. Everything hung up neatly on nails or hooks, sorted out in plywood boxes or shoeboxes. Wheels from toy automobiles, empty cans labeled *Rostock Fish Soup*, an indoor thermometer that points to eighty degrees Centigrade, shriveled tulip bulbs, a calendar page for the month of May 1956 showing a German woman embracing a Cossack, a baking tin, lid from *Polar Vanilla Ice Cream*, a bundle of *The Ladies' Hairdresser* magazines, a fur cap with only one earflap.

I hear her step behind me. I turn around. Her face, small as a shrewmouse's, has been ravaged by the wind and rain. Eyes and mouth are surrounded by a net of wrinkles. A face expressing awareness and friendliness. With eyes so blue and radiant they look like little pieces of sky in springtime.

Carefully, as though it were a mirror, she carries a huge picture in front of her. As she comes closer she says proudly, "Have a look. I'll hang it up here so everyone can see it."

She turns the front side of the picture toward me, propping it up on the toes of her shoes. Behind a huge crack in the glass I see the portrait of a red-haired lady. A string of pearls ornamenting her hairdo earned the painter's bitterest scorn. The same for the gem around her neck. Coquettishly the lady turns her eyes to the ceiling.

[2]

"Isn't that gorgeous?" whispers the Woodlouse. "They threw it out in the street, think of that. The children of Siebenschläfer around the corner, who died last week." She shakes her head and admires the picture anew.

Then she has a dust cloth in her right hand, polishing the glass around the crack.

After leaning the picture against the wall, she clears out the front side of the cellar passageway. The boxes marked *Dessert Eggs* VEB *Thuringia Chocolate Factory*,[2] piled up on the ruins of a shelf, she places in a nearby corner to the right. Takes down the flowerpots with sprouting leeks, the strips of cloth in lilac-green polka dots, and suddenly she has a pair of pliers in her hand, freeing the cracked masonry of nails and hooks. For this job she balances on a hunchbacked chopping block that she's scooted into place. She jumps down, steps back a few paces, examines the spot with narrowed eyes. She nods, climbs back up, pounds in a huge nail, yanks on it. It's far enough in.

Soon as she has both feet on the ground again, she lifts the picture warily, tries to climb up on the block. She groans, doesn't make it.

"Wait," I say, "I'll hold the picture."

She hands it to me, yanks on the nail once more before she takes it back again, and stretches in order to hang it up. The butcher's block tilts beneath her. Startled, I grab on, hold her firmly with both hands until her art work has finally assumed its place. While climbing down she says softly, "Thank you so much."

"Why do you do this anyway?" I ask. "Rummaging around all day in the wind and slush."

"Are the bottles, glasses, and boxes supposed t'just waste away?" is her decisive answer. "And besides . . . you can't just sit

2. VEB, an abbreviation for *Volkseigener Betrieb*, indicating that a firm or factory was state-owned.

still. Sit there and think: Ha, now I'm gettin' pension money,[3] when you've spent your whole life seein' that your kids get enough to eat. So I look for things to do. . . . My pension, actually it's enough . . . but I like to eat. Today I had beefsteak with cauliflower, yesterday Swiss rolls, tomorrow there's fish from the Market Hall. That's how it is. Besides . . . I have twenty-two grandchildren. You're surprised? But that's what happens with lots of kids, they have some too when their turn comes around."

Dumbfounded, I continue questioning.

"Oh no," she answers. "I didn't have all that many myself. Only five. Three are still livin'. Two died during the starvation years.[4] The others came with the men I married. There was a shortage of men after the war. For each one, four women. I was happy then that I got one again. Otto, my first, was killed in the last war. Johann had four kids. And then Gustav, after Johann died, had three. Now add 'em up, with my own. . . . Gustav didn't live long. Died from asthma he got here in the damp apartment. I caught some of it too. But no doctor can get a drier one for me. The housing office thinks: That old lady, she'll die soon anyway. . . . Sometimes I talk to the walls. . . . If I didn't have anything to do. . . . And my grandchildren, what would they get from me for Christmas then?"

A late evening. Beginning of September. I'm walking home from the theater. The fallen leaves the wind scrapes across the sidewalk sound like snail shells rattling over asphalt. A figure in front of me. Scurries to the building façade, presses against it. In a coat that looks familiar. And also the fur cap, the one earflap sticking out like a rabbit's ear. But no, her walk is different. Under

3. Retirement age for women in the GDR was sixty; for men, sixty-five. Any GDR citizen who had worked for at least fifteen years was entitled to a pension. The average monthly payment was relatively low, between 300 and 400 marks. However, old-age pensioners were provided with full insurance coverage and paid no taxes.

4. A reference to the hardships suffered by the German populace as the result of World War II.

her arm is a large bundle she clutches to her side as if she's afraid. Before she turns the corner, she stops, looks around. . . . The Woodlouse, stealing something?

Can't be, I say to myself. . . . And here? It's still a good hour's walk to our neighborhood. Then from a window a ray of light hits her, I see her profile with the small bumpy nose. A gate entrance swallows her up.

The next morning I carry the ashes down. She rummages as always in the cellar walkway. With an ax as big as she is, she's chopping up plywood boxes for firewood, stuffing it in sacks.

"Good morning," I call down to her. "Well, did you have a good night's sleep?"

She climbs up a few steps to see who's calling and says, as she discovers me, "Yes, very . . ."

A few weeks later, a freezing cold Sunday afternoon, my doorbell rings. A bit despondent, powerful at the same time, the way no one I know rings. She stands in the doorway. Shining white hair freshly washed. A smart dark blue dress with a starched white collar. She waits there, both hands holding up a big sack like a bouquet of flowers in front of her breast.

"I just want to bring you something," she says, reaching the sack toward me. "Dry branches and shavings for your stove. Because you helped me so kindly in the cellar the other day."

"Thanks," I say. "Do you want to come in for a cup of coffee?"

"But it isn't necessary," she says as she's already entering.

Then we sit opposite each other at the table. In the cupboard I also find half a Christmas fruitcake.

Our conversation is about this and that.

"Such a nerve," she says, in a voice full of sadness and faint anger. "In the front building, the beautiful banister. It's held up fifty years. But last night two posts suddenly disappeared. Simply sawed off for firewood. Now the banister shakes like a lamb's tail."

"Hm," I say. Stir around in my cup as if the hardest of sugar

[5]

lumps lay on the bottom. When after a while she becomes un-
easy, I say in a loud voice, "And what do *you* do during the night?"

She gives me a surprised look, picks every crumb up from her
plate, swallowing them with a show of pleasure. She pulls a big
checkered handkerchief out of her purse and wipes off the corners of her mouth. Then she sips on the coffee, wets her lips, and
begins with a smile, "I see . . ." She makes a serious face again and
asks me, "Haven't you ever seen the old lady Mothes, the really
old one who comes tottering in here every morning in slippers
that don't match?"

I remember. It was a short time ago in the cellar. I had my coal
bucket almost full, and I hear the strangest sounds in front of the
door. A shuffling and scratching, then mumbling. Startled, I
stand up straight. The light from the bulb in the cellar walkway
(that's been on since yesterday and, a miracle, hasn't been stolen
yet) outlines the figure of a tattered old woman some three
hundred years of age. Her bowed legs, thin as thread, are stuck
inside checkered stockings full of large holes. And these are stuck
into two mysterious slippers. A gray one made of felt, maybe a
size nine, with a tear in the middle that's been temporarily repaired with wire. And a brown one, still bigger, with a tassel. Her
body is enveloped in an ash-colored piece of clothing that in days
gone by must have been something like a coat.

"Mrs. Olschewski," says the figure without modulating her
voice. With a groan she holds out a bundle wrapped in brown
paper.

"I am not Mrs. Olschewski," I say, frightened, and, stepping
back, sit down on the coal pile. Picking myself up, I examine the
woman's narrow, shrunken face, her nose and chin sprouting out
like two needles. Her features are empty from years of waiting for
things that never happen. Her eyes fearfully wide open with a
look into nothingness.

"Mrs. Olschewski . . ." begins the voice again, "today . . . I've
brought a feather pillow."

[6]

I repeat that I am not Mrs. Olschewski and slap the dust from the seat of my slacks.

I grab my bucket and close the stall door.

"I see," she says slowly as she recognizes me. "Excuse me." Turns around and feels her way unsteadily back along the walkway, pressing the bundle to herself like a child.

"Yes," I say to the Woodlouse, "I saw her a short time ago."

"That's the wife of the bookkeeper Mothes. She's seen better days. Now she's ninety-eight and poor. Never worked, so gets only a small pension. Her three boys were killed in the war. She's got nothing left but all the books, ancient tomes. Then last week she says, 'You know what, Mrs. Olschewski, I'm going to open a bookshop. Emma Mothes' Bookshop.' I say: At your age! You can't manage that now, with the accounting and all the paperwork, and so on. When you're half blind. 'No?' she says. 'You don't think so?'" The Woodlouse takes another piece of cake, chews for a time, meanwhile staring at the wall as if a strange insect were sitting there.

"But's it's like this. . . . Yesterday, for example, she dragged in a comforter, a filthy thing from some rubbish heap. She almost got a hernia. Even the junk dealer wouldn't take somethin' like that. How she beamed. 'What you think it'll weigh?'

I gave her fifty cents as always. But where am I gonna put the thing? So I lug it to a trash container, one that's so far away she won't be pokin' around in it. And because she's out nights too, I have to be careful. For if she finds out . . ."

The Woodlouse bites her underlip, pulls out her handkerchief again and wipes the sweat from her forehead. Gestures with her right hand that the subject has been exhausted. Then she looks up at me again, blinking, as if she's about to ask: How's it going?

The Tall Girl

•

I

Manfred was twenty-one. He came to Berlin from his village in the Altmark.[1] After reading in the district newspaper that cement workers were needed for the housing construction program, he had asked his company to send him.

Once he'd arrived, he worked on the construction site of a cement plant. The others in his crew were approximately his age and liked him. He knew Ulli from their time together in the army, and the two of them shared a room in the employees' dormitory.

In his free time Manfred strolled through the city, looking at the people and the shops. Evenings he went with the others from his crew to their favorite bar. Except for Saturday, which was dance night in the *Kulturhaus* in Friedrichshain.[2]

Then Manfred said, "I'll stay here and read Cooper."[3]

Because he was lanky and a bit clumsy, he had a complex when it came to girls and dancing.

•

1. An area along the Elbe River near Magdeburg.

2. *Saalbau* or *Kulturhaus* in Friedrichshain (a borough of East Berlin). Operated by the state or one of the country's social organizations, houses of culture provided GDR citizens with both educational and recreational programs. Typically they consisted of a large hall and stage, a library, meeting rooms for smaller groups, a movie screen, and catering services. In 1988 there were more than 1,000 houses of culture in the country.

3. James Fenimore Cooper (1789–1851). Cooper's Leather-Stocking Tales were readily available in German translation in the GDR. They were especially popular among younger East German readers.

Baerbel was in her first year of apprenticeship, training to be a cook. Her mother ridiculed her choice of vocations. Baerbel, she thought, could have taken preparatory courses and gone to college.[4] Though Baerbel had really looked forward to her job, until now she had done nothing but trim the potatoes coming out of the peeling machine. She got bored.

She wasn't even allowed to go out dancing.

Ute, who sat next to her, was carving a potato to resemble a male figure with penis. "Come along tomorrow night," she said. "You're seventeen." She showed Baerbel her art work, then cut it in half and threw both parts into the pail.

Baerbel blushed.

"My mother . . ."

"Baloney, I'll call and tell her Saturday's my birthday."

"But you just had . . ."

"Does your ol' lady know that?"

"But would anybody dance with me?"

"There are tall guys, too, and if not, you can dance with me."

•

Saturday in the dormitory. Manfred lay on his stomach on the couch engrossed in a book. Ulli was shampooing his hair, getting ready for the evening.

"Manne, come along," he said as always.

Manfred had just finished *The Deerslayer.* There was nothing new left to read in the cardboard box under the bed.

"What's on the tube?" he asked.

Ulli threw him the evening newspaper.

"All junk," Manfred said. "What if I switch over to a West channel?"[5]

4. After completing the basic ten-year comprehensive schooling in the GDR, students could apply to continue in secondary school for another two years, one of the prerequisites for entering a university, or begin vocational training by signing an apprenticeship contract.

5. Up until the early 1970s it was illegal to watch television programs that originated in West Berlin or West Germany.

[9]

"Are you crazy? If they catch ya, you're through. Come on, we've got a table reserved. We'll have a few beers and check out the women."

II

Kulturhaus, Friedrichshain. In the space behind the dance floor the music wasn't quite so loud, people could still talk. Manfred sat at the table with Ulli and Bernd from his own crew and three young men from the neighboring crew. Between them were girls known to the others from previous nights.

"I'll stay on here a few more years," Freddy was saying. "When I've got a car and enough stashed away to buy my own place, I'll look for a softer job. . . . Come on, let's dance." He pulled a girl from the lap of his neighbor.

Two more girls came. A shorter one in jeans, wearing makeup like most of the others, and a very tall one in a bright summer dress. She looked around curiously. The shorter one knocked on the table.

"Hello, Ute," Ulli said, "what kinda giraffe ya got along?"

"Shut up, she's a buddy."

Manfred drank and listened to Ulli tell about their time in the army.

One of the young men instructed the tall girl to sit on Freddy's chair. "Otherwise ya block our view." He pulled Ute onto his lap.

Ulli got up to get more beer.

When he came back, he continued. "Manne really had somethin' happen to 'im. Tell about how ya lost your two teeth." He lifted Manfred's upper lip and pointed at the empty spaces to the right of his incisors.

"Come on, tell us!"

"Nothin' more to tell." Manfred waved them off.

Ulli talked for him. "Manne and Caesar and me got a citation, 300 marks and a one-day furlough. So we head for Warnemünde.[6] First a few beers. After that to the beach, up on the

---

6. A city in the extreme north of the GDR, on the Baltic Sea.

breakwater. It was March and cold. Then Caesar slips and falls into the water with his *felt uniform* on. It got waterlogged right away. Manne throws off his clothes, jumps in, swims over to Caesar and grabs him. But he was already goin' crazy, thrashin' around, and he hits Manne in the mouth. Manne spits his teeth out, pins Caesar's arm behind his back and paddles to shore. In the meantime, people are gatherin' around and start howlin' when Manne, naked, climbs outta the water with Caesar. I take his clothes over and say, 'Put 'em on.' But first he's gotta get Caesar breathin' again. And who shows up? The cops. They're goin' outta their minds. 'Taking off your clothes in public. This is no nudists' beach, and at this time of year.' "

"There's a guy fell in the water," I says. "He woulda drowned . . . 'Okay, but at least he should have kept his underwear on. That'll be 25 marks, causing a public disturbance . . .' "

They all laughed except the girl in the summer dress. She looked at Manfred admiringly.

"And did you pay?" she asked.

Manfred was too embarrassed to answer.

"Of course the man paid." Ulli shook his head. "I tell him, 'You should be gettin' the lifesaver's medal.' But him . . . always playin' the dumb guy."

More laughter, but the tall girl remained serious.

She had a round, childlike face.

What a post, Manfred thought. No one will ever dance with her.

Freddy came back. "Who took my chair?" The tall girl stood up. Freddy forgot what he was saying and stared. "Holy cow! And in high heels yet."

The girl justified herself: "My flats don't go with this dress."

"Then wear jeans," said Freddy. He stood next to her. "Without those stupid shoes you'd be exactly as tall as me." He plopped down on the chair. Manfred offered the girl his seat. She sat down.

Now there were no more chairs left.

"That's what you get," said Freddy. "Come on, big girl, that's Manne's place. Sit on my lap. I'm dancin' right away again anyway."

"Go on," said Ute, "he won't bite you."

The girl sat stiffly on Freddy's lap and held on to the edge of the table.

Freddy bounced his legs up and down. "Hey, she's really light."

Ute told the story of the invented birthday party.

"What's the matter with your old lady?" someone asked.

The girl was silent.

"Tell her she shouldn't worry about lettin' you go dancin'," Freddy said, putting his free hand around her waist. "This way you'll meet some guy and not be an old maid. Who'd want such a beanpole?"

"Shut your mouth," said Ute. "At least she's not as fat as you."

Everybody was dancing. Manfred and the tall girl sat alone at the table. She looked past him in the direction the music was coming from.

"What's your name?" Manfred asked.

"Baerbel," she said and beamed.

As Manfred thought over what he could ask next, Ute returned, looked disapprovingly at him and led Baerbel to the dance floor. She was really very tall, but her walk was smooth and erect.

III

The next Saturday Manfred was there again. Baerbel came in slacks and flat shoes. She looked a bit shorter and in general more attractive, nevertheless it angered him.

Freddy greeted her: "Tonight you're really all right. Duck your head a little bit and I'll even dance with ya." He pulled her toward the dance floor.

At the table the conversation focused on soccer, but Manfred listened to the music. Now they were playing a slow number. How do you dance to that, he wondered.

Manfred pictured Freddy's hands on the girl's hips. He waited a long time for the intermission but Freddy's and Baerbel's chairs remained empty.

When the music started up again, he walked toward the men's room, passing the dance floor on his way.

Freddy and Baerbel were dancing nearby, it was impossible to overlook them. They were a meter apart. Dancing alone with her eyes closed, she shuffled her feet and pumped her arms to the beat of the music, twirling around in her own circle.

Freddy moved stiffly and mechanically, grinning as he watched his partner.

"*All I Want Is You*," sang the guitarist and repeated it several times.

Manfred knew the song from a record and hummed along. In the men's room he looked in the mirror for a long time. He brushed the strands of hair away from his forehead. When he disregarded the two missing teeth, he thought his face was really all right.

Next week he'd make an appointment with the dentist, it had to be taken care of sometime anyway.

"And she says she's never been dancin'," said Freddy as Manfred came back to the table. He nodded in Baerbel's direction and wiped his forehead with his sleeve. "I thought she'd trip over her own feet, but uh-uh . . ." He patted her knee.

Manfred forgot to sit down.

Then Freddy went to the bar.

Manfred talked more than usual, looking at Baerbel in the meantime. She smiled but was hardly paying attention as she rocked her upper body to the rhythm of the music.

No one invited her to dance.

When they were alone, Manfred asked, "Wanna come along to the bar, have a liqueur?"

The girl shook her head, concentrating on the music.

After a while she looked at Manfred and asked, "Will you dance with me?"

Manfred saw how she blushed. He stood up and escorted her toward the dance floor. Baerbel was somewhat taller than he was but it didn't bother him.

A new number started up, a slow melody: "*For You . . .*" Manfred had never danced before. He looked at the others to see how they did it. He put his hand on Baerbel's shoulder.

Baerbel took his other hand in her left hand. She thought it was strangely cold.

"Just two forward, one back," she whispered happily. "Nothing to it."

Since Manfred was still standing in one spot, she assumed the lead.

He avoided her glance as he clumped all around her, stumbled over her feet. He clenched his teeth, but again he stepped on her foot. He regretted ever having entered the *Kulturhaus*.

Intermission. Manfred led Baerbel back to the table.

Ulli was surprised when he saw them coming. "Man, and he says he's never . . ."

Manfred sat down quietly and looked past Baerbel. Soon he left for the dormitory.

Maybe you aren't supposed to ask a boy to dance, thought Baerbel. She didn't look up as he left.

IV

Once again Manfred stayed in the dormitory on Saturdays. He sat alone in the television room or read. If somebody asked him what he'd seen or read, he couldn't remember. He worked as always, his shoulder blades moving as evenly as paddle wheels when he mixed or shoveled cement, but his mind was in the *Kulturhaus*. He clumped around Baerbel, stepped on her feet. . . . He wished to sink down into the cement or the mud, but he didn't.

Several times when Ulli came back from dancing, he was about to ask about her, what she had on, if anyone danced with her. He postponed the question until next time.

Sunday afternoons he walked up and down Prenzlauer Avenue, thinking she must live there.

•

Three months later he heard how they were teasing Freddy: "How's your beanpole doin'?"

Freddy swore.

A few days later Manfred asked Ulli, "Does the big girl still show up on Saturday nights?"

"Baerbel?"

"Yeah."

"She sure does."

"Anybody dance with her?"

"Once in a while Freddy is kind enough, sometimes somebody else. She thinks Freddy's somethin' great, God knows why."

From this point on Manfred started going home after work on Fridays. He put a new roof on the small house where his mother and younger sister lived. Saturday nights he went to the disco in the village inn, stood at the bar, drank beer, and chatted with old friends. Almost all were married and they asked, "What about you?"

He shrugged his shoulders. "I'm takin' my time."

Once when the band played *All I Want Is You*, he felt a pang of longing, but by the next number it was gone.

In October they often had to work overtime on the weekends, so he stayed in Berlin. Saturday nights he got bored. Finally he went with Ulli to the *Kulturhaus*.

v

Baerbel sat next to Ute.

She seemed different to Manfred. She was pale and the mascara under her eyes had smeared.

He asked himself what he had ever seen in her.

Freddy came from the bar. He belched, slapped Manfred on the shoulder and said to Baerbel, "Come on, dance time."

"I don't feel like it," she said.

"When I say dance, we dance!" Freddy pulled her chair out.

Baerbel stood up slowly and followed him.

When they came back she was crying.

Freddy took cigarettes and a lighter out of her purse and asked, "Anybody feel like comin' along t'get a drink?"

"Have one here," said Ute and shoved a glass toward him. "The bottle's for everybody." She poured him a glass of whiskey.

"Next to the crybaby?" Freddy laughed. "It's enough t'make ya throw up." He left quickly in the direction of the bar.

Manfred stared after him. He stood up, shouted out, "Freddy, set your ass down here!"

"Let 'em go," said Ulli. "If he sits here, it'll only get worse. Have a drink," he said to Baerbel and poured her glass half full. "You can handle that."

Baerbel did not react.

Someone said, "Did I ever tell ya about the time I went to buy a lampshade? My mother was havin' a birthday so I go into the CENTRUM department store.[7] She'd been wantin' a new shade for the floor lamp in the livin' room for a long time. Nearly impossible t'get 'em here. I go to the lamp section, but they only got shades for ceilin' lights. The clerk's busy with two customers wearin' fur coats. She's almost goin' outta her mind with 'Oh yes, Sir. Oh yes, Madam.' When she's finished, I tell her what I want. 'Don't have any,' she says and walks away. Just as I'm ready to take off, I spot shades for floor lamps back in the corner. The kind with gold trim. I ask the clerk, 'What d'ya call those back there anyway?' She looks me over, sees I just got off work, makes a face and says, 'They're really more for people with money, 200 marks

7. A large department store on Alexander-Platz, in the center of East Berlin.

apiece.' I tell her, 'Bring one of 'em over here,' and wave my bill-fold. 'I gotta little money myself.' You shoulda seen my mother's face."

"The clerk," Ute asked, "what kind of hair did she have?" She gave Baerbel a poke.

"Purple, some funny color . . ."

"And long earrings?"

"I think so."

"That's Baerbel's mother," said Ute.

Baerbel stared at the tablecloth.

Nobody laughed.

Then the others left to dance. Manfred and Baerbel sat at the table by themselves. She had buried her face in her hands and didn't look up.

After a while Manfred asked, "Don't you feel good?" Baerbel started up but didn't answer.

"Do you want to dance?"

She shook her head.

"You'd better go home," said Manfred. "I can see you don't feel good."

She seemed to think it over. "Yes," she said, then stood up, reached for her purse and left.

Manfred ran after her, took her by the arm. "You're really wobbly. I'll take you outside."

He helped her into her coat. Out on the sidewalk he asked, "Can you make it alone?"

She nodded. "Thanks," she said softly and walked away.

Manfred stared after her, then went back to his table inside the hall.

"Where'd the giraffe go?" asked Freddy.

"She got sick," said Manfred. "I sent her home."

Freddy shrugged his shoulders and headed for the bar.

"Why didn't you tell me?" Ute complained. "She can't go off by herself. . . . Has she been gone long?"

[17]

"What's wrong with her?" asked Manfred.

"She's carrying Freddy's kid, and it's too late for an abortion."[8]

Manfred noticed that the news offended him.

Then he asked himself, why shouldn't she have somebody's kid? What's it to you?

He turned to Ute. "Whatta ya mean, too late? And what's Freddy say?"

"He's already payin' for two kids," Ute said. "And at first Baerbel didn't want it either. When her mother found out about it, she called the hospital right away. Then Baerbel said no, just to show her. And now it's too late."

"And?"

"Her mother buttonholed Freddy, and when he heard that Baerbel stands to inherit a house in Binz[9] from her aunt, he said he'd marry her soon as the kid's born and he's plannin' to be a landlord up there."

VI

The following Saturday night Manfred appeared with a fresh haircut. He was wearing a suit, his only one, and a red polka dot tie.

Baerbel came with Freddy, she looked the same as she did the week before. Freddy brought over a Coke, took his cigarettes out of Baerbel's purse and disappeared. After a while he came back and pulled her out on the dance floor.

Manfred followed and watched them dance. Baerbel's movements were as tired and expressionless as her face.

A half hour later he and Baerbel were alone. He sat down on the chair next to her and started talking.

She was startled and appeared to notice him for the first time.

"Get away from him," Manfred managed to say. "I'll marry you.

8. A liberal abortion law passed in 1972 granted East German women the right to an abortion providing that it occurred within the first twelve weeks of pregnancy.

9. A popular resort town on the island of Rügen in the Baltic Sea.

"I'll adopt the kid, we'll move in with my mother in the Altmark. We have a house there. Please, get away from the guy."

Baerbel stared at him.

The dance was over, the others came back. Manfred stood up and said, "Think it over for a week. Next Saturday I'll be here . . ."

He left and during the following days felt calm. On Wednesday he wrote to his mother:

Don't be sad that I'm not coming home this weekend either. You see, I've got a girl here. You're surprised? I wanted to tell you long time ago, but you would have thought: only another false alarm. This time it's the right one. Her name is Baerbel and she's completely different from the others. I am very impressed by her, and I think for sure there will come a time when I'll love her. Next time I'll bring her along. By the way, she's no dwarf and no doubt will have to duck if she wants to get through the living room doorway.

Your son, Manfred

Saturday arrived. Manfred had even been to the dentist, the open spaces were filled.

There was nothing different about Baerbel's facial expression. "Hello," she said softly and sat down. Staring into her glass of cola, she seemed ready to fall asleep.

Then Freddy came, ordered her to dance. She followed him without a word.

Since Bernd had sprained his ankle at work and wasn't able to dance, Manfred had no chance to talk to Baerbel alone.

When she went to the restroom, Manfred waited for her by the coat-check door. As she came out, she almost collided with him. She drew back quickly.

"Oh, it's you," she said softly. She gave a little smile and started to go past him.

He caught her by the arm. "Don't you have anything to say to me?"

She shook her head and turned away.

Manfred stepped outside, breathed deeply a few times. He went back to the table and sat down opposite Baerbel. She acted as if he wasn't there.

Suddenly he blurted out, "Baerbel, I am serious. Get away from Freddy, I'll marry you."

It grew quiet at the table, somebody snickered.

"I'm telling you here in front of everybody."

Baerbel's eyes fluttered as she looked around the table, then she stood up.

"Where are you going?" asked Ute.

"To get some air."

"I'll come along."

Manfred wanted to join them.

"Keep your ass pinned right here," said Ulli. Loud enough so Baerbel could hear, he added, "Are you crazy? She's in the fourth month, and that brat of his'll be the same kind of cheat. Stuff like that's inherited . . ."

Half an hour later Baerbel came back with Ute. She saw the others gesturing to Manfred as they tried to change his mind. "Don't be stupid, Manne. Don't get yourself hung up . . ."

Manfred looked at Baerbel encouragingly. She did not react.

As the band played the final number, Freddy showed up roaring drunk. "Let's go, big girl. Home."

Baerbel stuck his cigarette pack in her purse, took out the token for their coats and followed Freddy to the coat-check.

Manfred hurried after them. He helped Baerbel into her coat. She thanked him and left with Freddy.

Manfred had to wait until he was handed his raincoat. He ran outside, Baerbel and Freddy had just turned a corner. He caught up to them and followed at a distance of three meters.

Baerbel walked hurriedly, Freddy stumbled after her and scolded. "Not so fast, whatcha been drinkin' anyway?"

Then they disappeared into a doorway.

Manfred noted the number and street. The next day he pestered his foreman until he was granted a three-day vacation, even though two of the other crew members were sick and another was in special training.

Monday morning at six o'clock he stood in front of the apartment house where Baerbel lived. She came out of the door at six-thirty. He went up to her quickly and said hello.

She said nothing and went on, he walked alongside her.

"I'm in a hurry," she said. They were almost running.

He leaped into the tram after her. She stood with her face to the window, the car was full.

Then he was walking alongside her again, trying to say something. She didn't listen.

Finally she disappeared inside a gate entrance.

Manfred just stood there, then he asked the doorman when the apprentices were through for the day.

The old man looked at him with a smirk and surprisingly gave him the information.

Manfred went to find a bar, but they were all closed. It occurred to him that it was still early morning.

In the dormitory he ate breakfast and lay on his bed waiting for the time to pass.

At four o'clock he stood across the street from Baerbel's factory.

Finally he saw her. She walked slowly, glancing to the right and left as if looking for someone.

As Manfred came up and greeted her, she blushed. In the tram he asked, "Are you that crazy about Freddy?"

She shook her head. "You don't even know me," she said.

Manfred laughed. "Better than you think," he said.

They got out. It was a cool, gray day in late autumn.

Baerbel draped her bag over her shoulder, stuck her hands in the pockets of her parka and walked next to Manfred. He began to talk, about his village, his childhood.

"I never had it that good," she said.

[21]

"Here there's no woods, no fields, no haybarns where you can romp around when you're a kid," said Manfred.

"I wasn't even allowed to play with the other kids in the back courtyard of our apartment building," she said. "My mother called them rabble."

He took her cloth bag and put his arm around her shoulder.

They walked down old, very narrow streets. The buildings looked like rotten tooth stubs. On the walls were ornately printed words: *Zimmermann's Ham and Bacon Processing, Ostrich-Feather Hats for Rent, Vegetarian Boarding House.* . . . The buildings had holes instead of windows. Behind many they saw faces, an old man wore a sleeping cap with a tassel on top that appeared to be hanging from only one thread. A young woman pushing her baby carriage came out of a doorway.

"What a difference it makes in Berlin," said Manfred. "A boy who likes to play with guns and give commands will be a gang leader here. If he lives in a highrise, Lenin Square[10] for example, he'll become an officer."

Manfred stroked Baerbel's parka where her belly must be. "It's gonna grow up in our village, okay?"

Baerbel smiled, she said nothing.

An hour later they came to a large square. They stopped at a café and ate ice cream.

In front of the door to her apartment house, Manfred said, "I'll pick you up again tomorrow morning."

"This was the most beautiful afternoon of my life," Baerbel told him.

VII

Baerbel's mother immediately scolded her for staying out so long.

Baerbel told her about Manfred. He was going to marry her, adopt the child, and they would move to the Altmark. Her mother lit a cigarette and laughed. She called Baerbel dumb

10. Located near the center of East Berlin in the borough of Friedrichs-hain. As a residential address, it connoted a privileged status within the GDR.

[22]

goose, little whore, and good-for-nothing. "Who'd want someone like you?"

Baerbel closed herself in her room and sobbed.

The next morning she left the house a half hour earlier. Manfred waited until around nine. He read the names on the mailboxes repeatedly, but he didn't know her last name. In the afternoon he waited in front of her factory. When she came out, she acted as if she hadn't seen him and walked very fast. As he caught up to her, she murmured "Oh hi," without looking at him or stopping.

He hurried alongside her, asking again and again what was wrong.

"Forget about yesterday," said Baerbel. She walked faster.

He followed her into the tram, but she turned to face the window. At her stop she squeezed quickly past him.

He waited two more mornings in front of her apartment building without meeting her. On Friday he rejoined his work crew. He was nervous, preoccupied. Had to smooth out a concrete slab three times before the foreman approved it.

The others poked fun at him: "He's got it bad for the tall one carryin' Freddy's kid around. . . . Come on, Manne, snap out of it!"

Manfred was also the target for ridicule and good advice when Baerbel sat with them at the table in the *Kulturhaus* on Saturday night.

She glanced at him once, apologetically it seemed, but she didn't dance with him. When Manfred left for the men's room, Ulli said, "Baerbel, leave Manne alone. Don't do him in. I'm divorced and I know what it's like. He's too good for somethin' like that. Isn't Freddy enough for ya?"

Baerbel stood up, took her purse and left.

On Monday Manfred stood outside her front door again. When she came out, he said, "Baerbel, I mean it seriously—"

She interrupted him: "I don't want to be married out of pity."

[23]

"But not out of pity, wait just a minute. You don't understand . . . I just admire how you—"

"Please leave me alone," said Baerbel. With a strangely proud look on her face, she walked past him.

Manfred quit work in the cement plant, packed his travel bag, and went home to his village.

VIII

A breakfast break on the construction site of the cement plant. "Did you guys hear about the tall girl who was supposed t'have Freddy's kid?" Bernd asked. "She did away with herself yesterday."

"The one Manne was keen on?"

"Yeah, jumped out a window. Fifth floor."

"But she was just at the dormitory yesterday afternoon," said Ulli. "She wanted to know where Manne lived. I told her, 'Not here anymore, took off.' 'Where to?' 'Home, in the Altmark.' 'And where exactly?' 'How do I know,' I says. 'Didn't leave any address. And anyway, you're supposed t'leave him alone.'"

"Idiot," said Bernd, "you could've gotten his address from the personnel files . . ."

"How am I supposed t'know she's gonna. . . . You only do that when ya got cancer or somethin'," said Ulli. Annoyed, he stood up and shrugged his shoulders.

Baerbel's funeral was on Saturday, the third of November.

Manfred has never learned of her passing.

Old Woman

•

I come back from vacation suntanned.

I ring the bell. No one opens. I ring again. Finally somebody comes shuffling along the hallway, the step so weary it doesn't sound like my landlady's.

My landlady, Mrs. Bernhard, a lively woman in her late sixties, writes all day untiringly on the second volume of her memoirs: about her time as a political dissident during the Nazi era. For the first volume she received considerable recognition.[1]

The door opens a crack. Frightened, I blink into the half-light of the hallway. Spot a figure lean as a rake, with pointed nose, sunken cheeks, large owl-like eyes that shine feverishly.

I hear, "Ah, it's you. Here you are. I've waited so long . . . here you are finally."

Before responding to her greeting, I stare at her.

Instead of the usual misshapen sweat suit she's wearing a new, very stylish pair of slacks and a yellow sweater. Both so full of cigarette ashes she looks as though she's covered with flour. Mrs. Bernhard after all.

Another long ash is about to drop from the cigarette in her outstretched right hand. As usual, I go searching for the ashtray.

"You're surprised, huh?" she stutters and glances down at herself, beaming. Then she taps her head and adds, "And a perma-

1. It was part of official GDR policy to deny responsibility for the Nazi era (1933–45) and to publicize the role any of its citizens may have had in opposing Hitler's government.

[25]

nent." She chuckles happily as I inspect the yellowish-gray curls of her hairdo.

She stretches out her arms, comes capering toward me. "And now I'll show you the whole apartment. You'll be surprised."

I set my bag down, plod after her.

The kitchen, normally reeking of dirty dishes, is unrecognizable. Everything is dusted, swept, polished. The new fluorescent bulb that stood packaged up in a corner for two years has been installed in the ceiling and gives off a dazzling white light.

"Now I can see the dishes much better," she remarks. "And over there," she points above the refrigerator, "I've fixed up a rack for the towels. Just now, still has to dry."

The hooks of the plastic rack point down like the prongs of a rake.

I clear my throat. Embarrassed and relieved, she explains the secret to me. "Last week I got the award.[2] And not one of my friends or comrades[3] came to congratulate me. But, you know, I figured out why. Even you don't stop in very often. And how were you supposed to feel comfortable in this place anyway? I should have noticed it sooner. Sticky cups and everything! And I . . . racked my brains for years, why . . ." She claps her hands, sways, and has to hold on to the table. "But now you're sure to come over more often, aren't you, for the news? Now that I don't look like a scarecrow anymore you'll come more often I hope. I was thinking you had something against our news.[4] That you'd rather watch the capitalists' television."

Her knees start to buckle, her eyes roll.

2. The specific award referred to is the government's *Vaterländische Verdienst Orden,* presented to East German citizens for serving their country in an exceptional manner.

3. *Genossen,* a term used to refer to members of the Communist party in East Germany, officially known as the Sozialistische Einheitspartei Deutschlands (SED) or German Socialist Unity Party.

4. A reference to the nightly news program on GDR television, *Aktuelle Kamera* (Live Camera).

I hold her up, try to move her in the direction of the bedroom. "Have you had your shot every day?" I ask.

"Oh, good Lord!" she says. "But I'll start again tomorrow."

She has diabetes. For more than ten years she has been painstakingly exact about giving herself shots regularly.

In the living room she yanks herself free. "I'm not sick!" She points around the edges of the carpet at the freshly painted floor. "You're surprised, huh?"

She heads for the table, holds a newspaper clipping up in front of me. "Last week . . . out of *New Germany*.[5] Isn't it good of me?" The photograph shows her with lips firmly pressed together, chin jutting out, and a look that blares like a fanfare. If I knew her only from the picture, I'd be afraid of her. She sighs. "I haven't done any work for three days. But tomorrow . . . tomorrow I'm starting a new chapter."

I take her by the arm, urge her to lie down. She whines like a child, pushes herself away from me and declares, "We'll drink coffee. The first visitor after my award."

Everything is set out on the white tablecloth.

With effort she unscrews the cover of the instant coffee jar, shakes coffee powder into each cup, and adds water from her thermos. She slides to the back of her easy chair, dangling her feet and beaming like a child under the Christmas tree. "The first visitor!" And after a silence, "But tomorrow . . . the chapter . . . you know, it begins like this . . . 'The small boy who plays alongside the wall where Rosa Luxemburg[6] is buried . . .'" She claps her hands.

Then she asks in a low voice, "Do you think they'll still come to congratulate me on winning the award?" Mrs. Bernhard gasps for

5. *Neues Deutschland*, the daily newspaper of the East German Communist party.

6. Rosa Luxemburg (1871–1919), a Polish-born political revolutionary who, along with Karl Liebknecht, founded the German Communist Party (KPD) in 1918. Assassinated in 1919, Luxemburg and Liebknecht were celebrated as political martyrs in the GDR.

air. I sip my coffee, the water is ice-cold and has not dissolved the powder. I set the cup down. Mrs. Bernhard shovels two spoonfuls of sugar into hers.

"Don't you use sweetener anymore?" I ask.

She looks at me in a puzzled way, slurps.

The telephone is in the hallway. Finding an excuse to step out, I call the emergency service.

As I come back into the room, she is stammering with her eyes closed. "I should've noticed sooner . . . such dirty cups, who'd want . . ."

I succeed in getting her into bed. She turns her face toward me and opens her eyes. "Surely you're still in the FDJ," she begins. "Why don't you wear your blue shirt more often?[7] I'd have it on every day . . . demonstrate what kind of socialist I am. . . . And in general I think you've once again . . . I looked around on your writing desk. One doesn't *read* something like that. I threw the book in the garbage. Yes I did. That's supposed to be a socialist writer? He's been bribed by the capitalists. You've got some hazy ideas. We have to discuss things again."

I turn aside. The book was expensive.

I look out the window. Evening is coming on.

"Will you visit me oftener, now that I've cleaned? . . ." Her voice quivers.

"Yes," I say, and think God forbid! From now on I'll sneak around in stocking feet so she can't hear I'm there and invite me over.

"Now I'll have guests oftener," she says happily. "The apartment. . . . Why, the young boy who—"

The doorbell rings.

7. Founded in 1946, FDJ (Freie Deutsche Jugend/Free German Youth) was a massive organization for young people between the ages of fourteen and twenty-five; it combined political indoctrination with leisure activities. During the 1970s and 1980s, membership exceeded 2 million, or more than three-quarters of all eligible young people in the GDR. To identify themselves, members wore dark blue shirts with an emblem of the rising sun.

"There is a flu epidemic," says the doctor, excusing herself for the delay. After she has examined the old woman, she telephones and says upon leaving, "Very serious. Diabetes coma. The ambulance is coming right away."

I pack Mrs. Bernhard's bathrobe, her toiletries, and a nightgown into a bag, set her purse containing her identification papers next to it.

Now she's sleeping, struggling hard for breath.

I remember a time our seminar group had gone on an outing to the Dresden Art Exhibition. I brought a catalog back, showed my landlady which pictures I thought were interesting.

She was thunderstruck. "You think something like that's good? A landscape full of garbage? In those colors? Since when is our reality full of garbage? And these haggard faces? What's the painter's name? Math . . . ?" She wrote down the name in her notebook. "I'd have it removed. On the spot. It imitates the pessimism that the capitalists. . . . That man deserves a rap on the knuckles. And you too."

I defended the painter.

She interrupted me in mid-sentence, scolded me. In reflecting upon Mrs. Bernhard, I wonder why she is this way.

Since I started shopping for her, she hardly left her apartment anymore. And when she did go out, she was picked up by a government car.

She tumbles out of bed. I run to the telephone, call the ambulance service once again and urge them to hurry.

A quarter of an hour later I call again, screaming into the receiver. The ambulance comes in five minutes.

A young, rosy-cheeked driver says with a yawn, "Couldn't make it sooner." Then as they are covering the old woman up on the stretcher, his partner picks up my landlady's things. The driver nudges him. "She don't need that stuff anymore."

The old lady whimpers. "No, my friend, just take the things along. I still have two volumes to write."

[29]

Then she almost manages to sit up, points threateningly in the direction of the window where a fat pigeon is pecking against the glass. "Hugo! It's not suppertime!" On the way to the ambulance she says, "Don't forget to feed the pigeons."

I promise not to.

The Attic

.

An old apartment house at the edge of a small town.

I climb higher and higher on a narrow, foul-smelling stairway, drawing myself in so I won't brush against the moldy wall.

The last floor. The nameplate I'm looking for is not here either.

I turn to the attic stairs. They groan under my step. The banister wobbles.

A crackling sound comes from the rafters.

Then I can make out two doors. On one of them a piece of yellowed pasteboard with ornate, faded letters.

I decipher *Eberlein*. My own last name.

I knock.

Finally I hear a voice within, creaking like the entire house. "Did someone knock, Augustine?"

"Yes, I think someone knocked," says another voice a bit more refined.

"Who is there?"

I shout my name through the door, adding, "I've just seen Aunt Liesbeth. I'm supposed to look in on you. She is sick and can't—"

"From Liesbeth!" shouts the more refined voice happily. "Where is the key, Minna?"

The door handle in front of my nose moves up and down in vain. The door is locked.

"Wonder where the key is, Minna . . ." Now the voice trembles with impatience.

"How am I supposed t'know?"

"But you were the last one outside. I slept 'til now, and before I fell asleep you went to the toilet."

"No I didn't. You had it last."

A squabble breaks out. "You have it!"

"No, you do!"

"Help, we can't get out!"

I wait, recalling once again my morning visit with Aunt Liesbeth in the hospital, how at the end, embarrassed, she had asked me: Could you drop in on my mother? She and her sister live around the corner from you, 13 Wilhelm Street . . .

They are supposed to be the sisters of my grandfather. And they live here?

Finally the door creaks open.

"It was in the coffeepot."

Two shriveled old ladies greet me. One of them calls me by my first name as if I am an old acquaintance. Doesn't her face resemble the strange, somewhat younger woman who always came to meet me on the bridge when I used to walk home from kindergarten or day nursery? Who stroked my head as she said, "Aren't you a pretty young girl," and stuffed my lunch sack full of candy?

"How nice of you to come!" she shouts.

The other one is still recovering from the excitement. She reports to me breathlessly, "There's such a gang of thieves in the building. They try t'run off with everything. That's why we always lock up. But they got into the storeroom anyway. One of the ten pairs of slippers disappeared . . ."

She swings her fist toward the floor.

"Ten pairs of slippers?" I ask.

"Yes, we bought 'em just last spring. Such beauties, with embroidery on the top. When somethin' comes along, you have t'grab it, right Augustine?"

"Yes," the other one confirms, a little embarrassed. "They're all

[32]

The Attic

a buncha thieves here. Two of the twenty-seven flour sacks are missing too . . . even though we always lock up."

They clear away tins and all sorts of junk from a kitchen chair, wipe it clean with the corners of their aprons. I sit down. Answer their questions about Aunt Liesbeth, and at the same time look around the room.

At the center are two rusty old sewing machines loaded down with strips and scraps of cloth in all colors. Between them a tall refrigerator, shabby white, standing on only three feet. I have the impression it totters under all its broken knick-knacks, shepherdesses, tiny angels, old pots, and cups, most of which have missing handles. A light clatter joins with the noise in the rafters. An unreal, discomforting singsong.

Opposite an open kitchen stove where a fire crackles I see pots covered with dust.

The low ceiling is black with soot.

The smell of burned milk comes surging toward me from the stove's corner.

I glance over at the windows. The sills are so crammed full it would be impossible to open one.

There is also a wall shelf with a bronze figure of an enraptured Jesus. And a badly worn sofa of green velvet.

Displayed on the wall above it, a large photograph of the old Berlin Palace ornamented with shiny gold paper inside a heavy frame. Thick cobwebs like rope ladders stretch from one corner of the room to the next. They encircle the lamp above me like a basket. Immersed in the half-light of evening, it all looks like a cave, a fox's den.

Yet nothing is able to outdo the peculiarity of the occupants who now, to the right and left of me, lean on the table and look me over with unconcealed curiosity.

"Yes, you'd be surprised at all the nice stuff we have," says the bigger one who is somewhat coarse. She is wearing a dirty apron and has a wiry gray brush of a mustache.

[33]

Full of cunning, her tiny eyes examine me.

Her sister, smaller, more delicately built, of a finer cut so to speak, smiles at me.

Her face, although shriveled like that of the other one, has something soft, girl-like.

She is wearing a brown knit sweater, halfway clean, with a large hole under the right arm.

Small golden rings with tiny diamonds sparkle on her earlobes.

"You're living in Berlin now, aren't you?" she asks softly. "Liesbeth told me. And you're going to college? I wanted to go to college too. Was always the first in school, right Minna? But we were five children and our father could afford the 3,000 marks it cost for only one. And one of us five was a boy, your grandfather. So he had to go to college and become a civil servant whether he wanted to or not. And I went out sewing . . ." She smiles.

The other one, her eyebrows raised, interrupts: "When there wasn't any cloth here, in the inflation time, we set out for Berlin too. First slaved away in a weapons factory, but that was nothin' for us. Then we got jobs in a honey factory. We stayed on there for two years, longer than any of the others. Because the work, it wasn't that easy. One time the director came over to both of us and said, 'Ah, the Eberlein sisters,' and even shook hands with us, right Augustine?"

She nods. "Yes, Berlin . . ." She glances respectfully over at the picture of the palace.

"But then there was cloth here again, and we headed for home."

The other one scratches herself on the nose with her long black fingernail, then asks confidentially, "How much you gonna earn after you graduate?"

I shrug, estimate a starting salary.

With shocked looks, they call out together: "You don't need to go to college for that. You can go sewing and make more."

I say something about the work also having to be fun.

They stare at me. The bigger one says, "But it's really money that counts."

Finally her sister admonishes her. "Be quiet, Minna. She already knows what she wants."

Minna doesn't stop shaking her head and murmurs, "Money's the only thing that shows who you are . . ." She rubs her thumb and forefinger together reverently.

I point to the ceiling and ask, "Don't you have a broom? I want to get at the cobwebs."

With some hesitation they hand me a broom that has only a few bristles left. I turn to the job.

The bustling activity startles them, but they calm down when they see the house isn't going to collapse.

The smaller one asserts for the hundredth time, "Oh, what a surprise to have you drop in on us. . . . You look exactly like your dad. Yes, your dad. He used to run after us like a little puppy when he was five. We always stuck a piece of sugar in his mouth. Then he'd laugh. And now he doesn't even know us anymore. Since he married your mom, he's ashamed of two old maids . . ."

"No, no," I say, embarrassed. "It's only that he's very busy. Never has any time at home either."

The bigger one pokes her sister in the side. "Psch! What if she tells him?"

They change the subject. "Should we . . . should we show her our dowries?"

They rummage out a key from the cupboard. Then they walk solemnly toward a door that must lead to their bedroom.

They come back, their arms full of boxes and packages, and pile everything up on the couch. After running excitedly back and forth many times, they start unpacking. Then they call out, "Look!"

I set the broom in the corner behind the stove, wash my hands in the sink, secretly wipe them dry on my slacks and turn my attention to the hosts. It is astonishing.

A stack of the finest linens with embroidered monograms A.E. and M.E., paper-thin porcelain dishes that are hand-painted, sets of silverware. They sparkle in the room's dull light.

I take up a plate in my hand, examine it.

"It's from Bohemia," Augustine explains to me. "Old Fanny, my friend brought it out. In a backpack, fifty of 'em. And not a one got broken on the way. That was sixty years ago. . . . Look, this is the prettiest one. You know what? I'm going to give it t'you because you've come to visit us."

The big one is startled, then she appears to work up the courage. After wiping her hands nervously around on her apron, she says, "Here, I'll give you one too. We're gonna buy some new ones again. The times are better now. The stores have somethin' in them and we grab what we can . . ."

She scurries to the kitchen cupboard, fetches wrapping paper and a roll of string. "We'll wrap 'em up good for you so nobody sees 'em on the street. Thieves are all over the place."

"Such large dowries," I say. "Why didn't you get married?"

Silence.

The smaller one looks at her sister encouragingly. "We can tell . . ."

The bigger one wheezes, lays her things on the table, glances down at them uneasily. "Engaged . . . yes, we were both engaged. . . . But it was like this. My fiance, he was . . . ya, actually he wasn't a bad human being. From out there where the Catholic church is, that's where he came from. But during the bad time, when there was nothin' to eat,[1] he climbed over peoples' garden fences and brought back a sack of apples for us every night. Until he got caught. Then had to go to jail. Couple weeks before the wedding . . ."

She swallows, breathes a sigh of relief. "Came just at the right time. Otherwise I'da brought a thief into the family."

The smaller one adds, "We come from better stock. Our father was the master baker. What would people have said?"

---

1. The late 1920s.

"When he came out of jail," the bigger one continues, "he was standin' outside our door again. Our mother was horrified. I chased him away. 'Don't come around here anymore. A man who's done time, pfui!'"

"In my case it was this way," Augustine begins slowly. Her face twitches. "He wasn't a bad human being either. The son of the Rösslers, the ones who had the construction company. For three years we got along fine with each other. But . . . he couldn't wait 'til the wedding. He'd already had his way with me. What did I know about such things? And all of a sudden Liesbeth arrived. Mother shouted, 'For heaven's sake, what a rotten man! Sticks you with a kid before the wedding!' And I said to him, 'You rotter, I don't want to see you anymore!' After that he often came back again, looked at Liesbeth so and still wanted to marry me. But I said, 'Get out of here, I'll raise my girl alone. Everybody'll see I can do it by myself.' I had my pride too. And didn't I raise her? She hasn't wanted for a thing. And when I'm no longer around, she inherits it all."

With a devout gesture she points over at the mountain of dowry goods.

And this morning I had visited Aunt Liesbeth in the hospital, an old woman and deathly sick.

"And Augustine was a real beauty," the bigger one continues. "The prettiest in the whole village. In comparison I looked downright ugly. And the way she dressed." With a gesture she shows how one adjusts a splendid hat, big as a wagon wheel. "And this is the way she'd hang the little purse on her arm." She demonstrates. "Everybody turned around to look at her. . . . But you see, she didn't have any more luck either. What's the use of bein' a real beauty?"

Something flashes in her eyes, a combination of sympathy and boastfulness.

Augustine nods sadly, and at the same time there is something else in her eyes. Pride? Stubbornness? She says, "Yes, I was a beauty. Lots of men wanted me later, too. But I told them, 'I have a girl at home that I'm going to bring up. And she'll inherit what I've got. I'll be Miss Eberlein until I die.' You have your pride, after all. And if you've been so disappointed once, you don't want to start up with anybody else."

"Even two years ago," her sister remarks, "some man was following her around town. . . . Tell her about that, Augustine."

"Yes, he toddled after me through the whole town. He's seventy at most, I was thinking. And when he actually spoke to me, I told him what I told all the others . . . that I'm already going on ninety, but I'm the only one who knows."

"I have to leave," I say. "Maybe I'll visit you again sometime."

They pack up my plates ceremoniously. "This is good string, from the early days," explains the one. "Old Fanny gave it to us for Christmas. She was dressed up as Rupperich,[2] but we recognized her anyway. By her voice."

When Augustine sees me staring at the picture, she smiles and says, "Ah, yes, the Berlin Palace. Were you ever inside?"

"That hasn't been there for a long time," I say. "It was bombed out and then torn down after the war. Marx-Engels Square[3] is there now."

She looks at me with widened eyes, her face turning a doughy yellow. She doesn't hear my good-bye.

She stands looking up at the picture, her mouth quivering.

The other one accompanies me to the door, turns on the attic light. Before I leave, she sweeps her tongue across her parched lips, winks at me slyly and whispers, "When you start earnin' money, don't keep it only in *one* bank. Better in two or three. If one of 'em goes broke, you still have somethin' in the other one."

I thank her and hurry down the stairway.

2. A reference to Knecht Ruprecht, a legendary figure who accompanies Nikolaus (St. Nicholas) at Christmas time.

3. Marx-Engels-Platz, a large square just off the avenue Unter den Linden near the center of East Berlin.

Construction Site: A Documentary

.

I

Beginning of March, 1973. A flock of crows whirred about the
sun as it crept up behind the woods on the opposite shore of the
river Spree.

Shivering, I stood and watched.

The river in front of me was like glass. Seagulls perched atop
the posts sticking out of the water looked as if they'd been
stuffed.

I turned around: cranes, huge cement trucks a dirty orange
color, pieces of iron, mud. . . . Not a soul. It was the breakfast
break.

A few days before, in high spirits, I had gone into the personnel division of the VEB Construction Combine[1] and said, "I want
to go to a construction site . . . no, to actually work. On shifts too.
Yes, I have a degree, but only school and studies all the time.
What do I learn from that?"

Finally they hired me for construction work at the cement
plant. And now here I was.

I turned toward the tall building where I was supposed to
meet my crew.

Room 312.

The door to the room needed repair. There was only a hole

1. *Kombinate* (combines) were the largest economic units in the GDR,
employing some 40 percent of the work force. The abbreviation VEB indicates
that it is state-owned (see note 2 of "The Woodlouse").

where the handle and lock should have been. Voices came from the other side.

"Gonna take it?"

"Hey, sleepy, I asked if you was gonna take it."

"Help, he's takin' my king."

"Not so loud, damn it. What's the time? . . . By the way, somebody new's comin' today. Someone educated . . ."

I stayed outside.

"Educated? What's he want here?"

"It's a she."

"What? A broad?"

"Zappe's got three women in his outfit too."

"Those with Zappe ain't women, they're tanks."

"One time we had two educated ones on a buildin' job. Wanted t'earn some extra cash supposedly. We could understand that. But those two! They didn't jus' look around, they gawked like they was at the zoo. After four weeks they'd had enough. And what was goin' on? They had t'write an article about *The Working Class.*"

"And why are we gettin' this one? We'll have t'do her work for her."

"Wait a bit, maybe she's a tank too."

I knocked.

Somebody whistled as I entered.

"A tank!" one of them shouted.

A tall, haggard man, the only one with a haircut you could call passable, turned to face me. "So, you are . . ." and he said my name. On the table in front of him lay a notebook and eyeglasses.

"Yes," I said.

"This is my crew: Bummi, Kalle . . ." and he called out five names.

"I'm the foreman, Werner."

The faces resembled each other. They had been toughened by exhaustion and the weather. The foreman shook my hand. As I made the rounds, the others extended their little fingers.

One was asleep. His head lay directly on the table.

"Hey, the new one," shouted his neighbor and poked him before addressing one of the others. "No cheatin', spades are trump. One more time and you're playin' alone."

The one just awakened had tired, puffy eyes. He meant to reach his little finger toward me, looked at me thoughtfully for a minute and stuck out his hand. "Lo, I'm Knolle."

His hand was hard as a piece of wood.

I said, trying to be brash, "I thought there were more of you. . . . Is this the entire crew?"

"Aren't all here," said Werner sullenly. "Two in training, one sick, one still comin'. We call him 'the Retiree.' The guy gets sick from every little breeze."

The door opened.

"Speak of the devil and here he comes," said Werner. "Well, Retiree, feelin' better? You're here early."

The latecomer was a tall, heavy-set boy of eighteen or nineteen. "Mornin', my alarm clock didn't go off . . ." he stuttered.

No one paid any attention to him.

"My trick!" Kalle slapped a card on the table.

The boy stuck his hand out to each of them. "It wasn't just a cold, my tonsils too . . ."

Without looking up, each of the men held out the tip of his little finger.

I offered him my hand, said my name.

"How much ya got, Bummi? Forty-eight? Man alive, and then ya pass? Ya don't pass with that! Just don't play in the bar. Anybody'd nail ya right away. And I saw your cards long time ago."

"Forget it," someone said. "We all have to start sometime. Let's go, deal 'em out again, Bummi."

The speaker had a strong lisp. His fire-red hair, sticking up like a plume, set him apart from the others.

Werner turned to me. "You get a locker next door. You can

shower and change over there. The stock-keeper in the base-ment'll give you your equipment and a padlock for your locker. And make sure you get plenty of soap paste. After work you'll be dirty as a pig."

I pulled the door shut behind me, heard from outside, "She won't last long."

I took the stairs down two at a time, relieved, God knows why, in thinking I'd arrived at a place where everyone speaks his own mind.

II

"Knolle, go ask if the horseshit concrete isn't comin' soon. . . . It's never the same here," the foreman explains to me. "When there's no concrete, we stand around. When it comes we work like idiots. We pour ten forms every shift, and the two special slabs over there . . ."

I took a few steps in my huge rubber boots. My work jacket was also three sizes too big. Trees prickly and bare lined the longer sides of the site. Gusts of wind tugged at them.

I wrapped myself in my work jacket.

After one hour I started treading on my own feet in order to keep my toes warm.

A baldheaded man in his early forties approached the group. Werner turned toward him. "Come on an' eat breakfast with us. No use sittin' alone back there."

Bravely, I stepped up too. The others didn't seem to notice. "This is our crane operator for now," Werner explained to me. "Our old one got beat up night before last. In Friedrichshain, skull fracture."

"His own fault," said the tallest and brawniest one in the group. "I don't get mixed up with crazies like those. Man, I clear out."

Knolle came back and reported: "The concrete's comin' in ten minutes."

Bummi, the apprentice, turned to the crane operator. "Why d'you shave your head anyway?" he asked.

The latter calmly finished his cigarette, threw the butt in the nearest puddle and asked back: "And why d'you have such long curls like a woman?" He grinned. "I use t'have mine that long too. And a full beard. So no one 'ud recognize me. I got in a jam. Was on probation for a year, sweepin' streets in my own neighborhood. Same place I was a clubhouse director[2] at night. When my time was up, I had everythin' shaved off again. But that's how I learned what kinda curls I got. Fiery red and frizzy as mattress stuffing. . . . Comparin' 'em, I like this better." Tenderly he passed his hand over his bare skull.

"Let's go!" Werner shouted suddenly. "Cigarettes out. Vibrators[3] over here. Where are they, anyway? Hurry up, where are the vibrators? Yeah, for the others too."

He grabbed a shovel, threw a second one over to me.

I stared at the cement truck that crept toward us, snorting like something primeval.

Around three o'clock I dragged myself home, my back aching. After the clatter of the construction site, my own street seemed spookily empty. A man with a poodle in a knitted jacket came toward me.

The clock in the Church of St. Sophia struck quietly. I heard it for the first time.

I fell into bed. Around midnight I woke up. My stomach sounded like a frog pond. I hurried into the kitchen and saw that I'd forgotten to buy groceries. Refrigerator and bread box were empty. I found two cans of mackerel filets in mustard sauce. I wolfed them down, drank my fill of tap water, and went back to sleep.

The alarm clock rattled. It was pitch dark. I remembered that I'd set the alarm for ten minutes earlier than the time I had to get

2. As a clubhouse director, the crane operator would have been responsible for organizing cultural and recreational activities, most likely for young people.

3. A vibrator is a tool for compacting concrete by vibration before it has set.

up. With some effort, I rolled over. Outside it was raining. The drops pounded against the metal plate beneath the window. I bolted up, switched on the lamp on the nightstand and stared at the clock. Ten minutes more. With half my mind I was counting the seconds, and with the other half I was at the construction site. A blaring and roaring, the sky like the ceiling of a smokehouse. In my hands the vibrator. I hold it up with all my strength, shove it into the concrete once again. Finally loosening up, the concrete crowds into the openings of the steel net. I yank the vibrator out, and it bangs against the ground. As I'm about to turn it off, I hear: "Leave it on, keep at it. When you're finished, the special slabs are over there . . ."

I shovel the surplus concrete into a wheelbarrow, pull it over to the forms for the sidewalk slabs and take up the vibrator again. I shovel, vibrate, shovel. . . . The vibrator, the wheelbarrow, the scoop, the hand float, the vibrator, the wheelbarrow, the scoop. . . . Then I no longer feel my muscles, my mind is gone. I bolt up again. Still five minutes.

Relieved, I sank back down. The dream continued. Side glances. "Well, pipsqueak, ain't ya callin' it quits soon?"

I feel my every move and every breath is being examined mercilessly. I hurry along the forms, a float in my hand. It's like running the gauntlet.

I glanced at the clock again, still three minutes. I'm getting fidgety, feel a gooey mixture of oil, concrete, and sweat pressing through my pants leg. The same on my face. I have no time to wipe it off. Someone whispers, "Ya get paid extra for that, a dirty-work bonus."

Two more minutes . . . I curled up under my quilt. I hear a voice behind me, "Hurry up, Retiree. Still not done with the eyelet holes? Look at the new one, the way she jumps up and sets to it. She's only a fourth your size."

I threw the covers off.

[44]

III

We had lined the forms and were standing around waiting for the concrete. The others were smoking. The night before they'd been at the bar and were still half asleep. It was raining. The drizzle came down like tiny pins.

"Let's go, Bummi," said Knolle. "Get the eggshells."

Bummi trotted off to get the helmets.

It was still pitch dark.

We pressed the helmets down on our foreheads. At least they provided a small roof.

A man in street shoes came toward us. He hopped across the puddles, pulling up his pants legs as he went.

A green notebook was wedged under his upper right arm.

"The manager," Werner explained to me.

He stopped two meters in front of us, made a bigger leap over the last puddle and almost landed on Knolle's boots. Knolle didn't budge. The manager took half a step backward and stood on tiptoes in the puddle.

"Morning." He looked at each of us.

There was a mumbled reply. Only the Retiree answered with proper respect.

"You're the new one, aren't you?" the manager asked me.

I nodded and said my name.

He opened his notebook and after stepping up right next to me, thereby winning dry ground, announced: "Workers' Safety Instructions."

He wrote down my name, then instructed me: "Helmet, . . . under suspended loads, . . . report accidents immediately, . . . no alcohol." He handed me the ballpoint pen.

I didn't react. Werner tapped me. "Put your John Henry at the bottom."

My signature looked weak and forlorn among the flourishes of the others.

The manager went hopping off, his pants legs splashed up to the knee.

[45]

Somebody snickered. "He's gotta tie on under his work jacket."

"Not even the director's like that," added one. "At least he shows up here in boots."

Out in the cold the Redhead's lisp was stronger than usual: "The managers, forget it. Think they're somethin' special and mornin's they don't show up theirselves 'fore five."

"How come you're makin' such a funny face?" Knolle asked me.

"Because of the bottle," I answered. "I've got a bottle of schnapps in my locker, to celebrate my new job with everybody.[4] And now I hear alcohol isn't allowed."

Laughter.

Someone poked me on the shoulder. "Lotta things aren't allowed. Besides, who's gonna see it?"

I was shivering.

Werner looked at his watch and swore. "Now I'm gonna go see what's happened to that shit," he said. He ran off toward the mixer, came trudging back exhausted. "Short on vehicles today. Not until after breakfast. So let's sweep up some trash."

The others objected. "In this weather?"

"Well, all right," he conceded. "It's dark enough, they can't see much from up there." He pointed at the office building. "But go stand behind the slabs."

It rained and rained.

I kept looking at my watch. Still an hour until breakfast. Still fifty-five minutes, still fifty-three . . .

Werner held a package of cigarettes in front of my nose. "Here, have one."

"I really don't smoke," I said. I was embarrassed, ready to be laughed at.

"That's smart," the crane operator said and took a deep drag.

"Yeah, smokin's horseshit," said the tall, brawny one.

4. *Einstand*, a German custom that calls for a new employee to share a bottle of schnapps with fellow workers.

[46]

"Whatcha supposed t'do, standin' around all the time? At least *somethin'*."

Werner waggled his cigarette between his thumb and fore-finger skeptically. Then he struck a match in the hollow of his hand and said, "Yeah, don't pick up the habit."

A month later I was smoking with all the rest of them.

To ward off the cold, I kicked one foot against the other. My socks and work boots felt damp and sticky.

"Freezin'?" asked a tough little man called Joe. "Yeah, this drizzle shit. It's worse than ten below in the winter time." He sniffed the air suspiciously. "March already, and still no sign of spring."

"November'll be here first," said Knolle.

Werner tried to cheer us up. "You're gettin' paid for this. Would ya rather go inside, settle for less?"

A bowlegged man came slogging up in muddy boots. "Morn-ing! How's it goin'?"

"The foreman from next door," Werner explained to me. He pointed to the paved road nearby, where I could see a row of shadows perched on the jaws of a crane.

"How's it goin' with you?"

"Terrific. Head's all clear. Haven't had a drink for a whole week. Not a drop."

Someone guffawed. "I know how that goes. But it starts build-in' up. One, two more days and you'll be droopin'. You'll toss down a beer, then another, and then . . ."

"You wait," said the man. "Just wait." He didn't sound very con-vincing.

"You're the new one?" His grip hurt my hand.

"You're supposed t'come upstairs, payroll office. Fourth floor. Bring your papers. Job contract and stuff."

I ran toward the warmth and light and was disappointed when everything was taken care of so fast.

"Pay day is always on the twenty-first. It's almost that now," said a plump lady in her fifties. "You'll get paid some already." She smiled at me. The smile made me feel good.

The hallway glistened. Many large potted plants. I read the nameplates next to every door: Production Manager, FDJ, Head Machinist. There wasn't a sound. I walked along cautiously. Then I looked down at myself and thought, at least no one can tell I'm "the new one" anymore.

A noise behind me. I turned around. A middle-aged employee, wearing an apron on top of his work clothes, was bent over following my zigzag trail from door to door, a wet rag in his hands.

"Can't you wipe off your feet?" he grumbled as he caught up to me.

Surprised, I asked him, "Do you always do this?"

"Always. New here, huh? I've got a job restriction, doctor's orders." He grinned. "This way I put my time to good use 'til retirement." With a groan he rose up, glanced at his apron. "Yeah, I look like a woman. But at least here I'm not killin' myself. And I keep my full salary . . ." His entire face lit up, as if his illness were a blessing of fate.

A door opened in front of us.

Pushing his way out backwards, the Retiree spoke hurriedly into the room. "Yes, it'll be great, about partners in arms. . . . And somebody has to do it. . . . The last one was in December."[5]

"Fine, fine," a calm voice interrupted him, "go right ahead."

The Retiree made half a bow, closed the door and almost stumbled over us.

His face reddened, then he said, "The bulletin board, I have to . . ." The door opened again. A tall man stepped out, his expression one of decisive mildness, if one can call it that. He intended to pass by, then his glance fixed on me. "How do you

5. Bulletin board displays in the work place, in this case on the theme of "partners in arms," were most often used to promote the political aims of the Communist party in the GDR.

do," he said, offering me his hand. "I'm the director, Wittmann. Well, how's it feel to be working?"

I answered evasively.

"Yes, a tough job, but your crew is our best one. He turned to the Retiree. "Will the bulletin board be ready today?"

The Retiree marched off like a soldier.

The man with the floor rag had also left.

"If the concrete came on schedule," I said, "it would be easier. We still haven't gotten a load today."

The director looked surprised. "But they reported to me . . ."

He promised to check into it right away.

I went back to my crew.

Somebody asked if I'd seen the Retiree.

"Yes, he's making up a display for the bulletin board."

Werner spit. "Must have gone beggin' to Wittmann. He'll never be a construction worker."

"Just wait," someone said, "he'll be givin' orders to all of us. I can smell it comin'."

The rain had let up, but new storm clouds were drifting in.

Finally we had a break for breakfast.

Outside the door of the canteen there was lots of commotion where a line had formed.

"We're the last ones again," said Bummi. "Tomorrow we're comin' early too."

I was shocked at what my fellow crew members gulped down. For Knolle I counted seven bread rolls, thickly spread on both halves. On top of them he poured down four bottles of soda. Joe, who had put away ten rolls, wiped his mouth with his jacket sleeve and belched loudly.

The tall, brawny one yanked his sandwich away from the table. "The pig, he'd spit right in my food!"

"You do that at home too?" asked Werner.

"Sure, after a meal everybody belches."

[49]

The tall one went right at him. "That's what you think! We're not pigs here." He looked ready to grab Joe by the neck.

Joe took a deep breath and, in a voice I hadn't expected, bellowed: "Shut your traps! What about last night in the dormitory, huh, big guy? Remember how you slurped? Slurped and belched and all but shit in my soup!"

Bummi raised his arms to shield himself.

"I slurped, yeah, but I never belched," the tall one responded.

Werner confirmed it. "No, he didn't belch. You're the only one who does. We've been listenin' to it for a year now. I don't have nothin' against slurpin', that means ya like the soup. But belchin' is outta line."

Joe started waving his arms. "Shut up, all of ya, goddammit!" He jumped up and headed for the door, slamming it behind him.

Ten minutes later he was back, sitting down calmly with the rest of us.

I thought it was time to fetch my bottle of schnapps out of the sink, where I'd put it under cold water.

I opened it up, set it on the table. "My treat!" No one touched the bottle. They were looking out the window at a flock of crows that flew up behind the woods at just this time every morning.

One of them stretched his hand out toward the bottle but drew it back. "No glasses."

Werner directed Bummi to get some tea mugs from the canteen.

Bummi didn't move. "Aren't any more of 'em left."

"How 'bout a little game?" asked the baldheaded crane operator. He pulled a badly worn deck of cards out of his pants pocket.

"Why do we need glasses?" I asked. "Let's drink out of the bottle." I took a swig and passed it to Knolle. He took several big gulps and handed it over to Bummi. The bottle made the rounds. At the end there was still a swallow left for me.

"Hits the spot." They were licking their lips.

[50]

"Why're you here, anyway?" asked Knolle. "You got an education, there's easier ways to earn your dough."

Werner changed the subject. "Tomorrow some guy from the newspaper's comin'. And the day after is an FDJ meeting.[6] Nobody go runnin' off after work."

"Gonna be in the newspaper?" The crane operator stuck out his lower lip. "Ya let 'em do that to ya? Don't be stupid, I know what I'm talkin' about . . . '61, I was doin' my army time. A newspaper guy comes over, asks me what I think about the Wall goin' up, the 'political measures.' First thing that comes t'mind, I say, is it use t'take me ten minutes by tram t'get to my job in Berlin. Now I hafta make a huge detour an' it takes me an hour. Next day the newspaper has me sayin' that I think we shoulda had the border a long time ago. The last part went, 'Once again we have called imperialism to account.'[7] Supposed t'be my opinion. When I went back to my unit the next day, you shoulda seen how they looked at me . . . they never took me serious any more."

"What're we supposed t'do?" Werner mumbled. "They come anyway, even if we say no."

"And another meeting?" somebody complained. "Horseshit! Meetings, meetings . . ."

"And I've got job trainin' besides," said Knolle.

"Why ya wanna be a foreman? You'll be goin' to meetin's the rest of your life," said Joe.

"What? He wants t'be a foreman? . . ." The crane operator made a face. "As if ya can't earn your money jus' workin'. And you guys put up with all this meetin' stuff? I seen right away you're a buncha country boys. Somebody should try that with us. At our place ya won't find a soul after two-thirty. And if the Emperor of China . . . ah well, a model crew."

6. The FDJ is the abbreviation for Free German Youth, a political organization in the GDR; see note 7 of "Old Woman."

7. The crane operator is recalling the construction of the Berlin Wall in August of 1961 and the political propaganda that accompanied it.

"I can't make it," said Joe. "My day off for household chores. Lots of laundry."[8]

Calmly Werner unfolded a technical drawing, pushed the soda bottle aside, and after he had carefully wiped off his hands on his pants, spread the drawing out over half the table. He took his glasses out of the case, put them on and bent over the drawing. As if it were an afterthought, he said, "Don't talk garbage. You'll all be here. This is the new kinda slab we have to pour."

I had purposely ignored Knolle's earlier question. Now I described my meeting with Wittmann and said he wasn't aware that we didn't have any concrete.

Werner shrugged his shoulders. "I tell the manager, he tells the shift engineer, and on up it goes."

"To the government head," Bummi added.

"Six weeks ago," said Joe, "the director announced his inspection on a day when there wasn't no concrete delivered. We're eatin' breakfast and in comes Siedow, the production manager. Says we're supposed t'stay inside, an' you shoulda seen the sunshine! Then he asked what we had left t'do. 'Restack the U-parts,' we said. 'How long will it take?' 'Half an hour.' 'Good. Stay put and eat your breakfast 'til you hear from me.' Fifteen minutes before the director's comin', Siedow shoos us down there. Then when the boss shows up we're busy restackin', and the crane's swingin' back and forth. Nobody standin' around—"

Werner interrupted him. "But on the days right after that there wasn't any problem gettin' concrete."

"That's a long time ago," said Joe.

I was getting excited. "Then we've got to wake them up. If ten managers can't see to it that we get concrete, we'll have to do it ourselves. For example, one of us is stationed at the mixer. Just see what comes out. We're the working class, we pay the office guys' salary." In concluding, I said: "I'm the one responsible for

8. At this time only married women in the GDR work force were entitled to one day off a month for household duties. Obviously the male speaker knows this.

the newspaper business. A girlfriend of mine works for *Young World*,[9] in the department called Youth of the Working Class. She wants to interview us." Just as I was saying, "We can bring up the stuff about the concrete, . . ." Werner yawned and the others stood up without looking at me.

IV

The concrete arrived on schedule during the rest of the day. Thus my remark to Wittmann hadn't been in vain.

But my feeling of satisfaction over it was spoiled by the looks I got from all sides. They seemed to be asking, haven't you had enough yet? Yesterday they'd given me little chance, now none at all.

Presumably they were watching for a sign of exhaustion. I shoved the vibrator into the form filled with concrete, vibrated through two forms, scraped the leftover concrete together with my last ounce of strength, and then somebody smacked a hand float down in front of me.

The day before I'd watched them smoothing out the concrete, now I tried it myself. The float stuck to the damp mass, continued to dig up new holes.

I decided to ask someone for help. They stood nearby, smoking. As I drew close, I heard the crane operator. "Naw, I been workin' ten years on construction, all over hell . . . but I never yet heard such a bullshitter, even if it is a broad . . ."

Without asking anything, I went back and took up the hand float again.

I heard the crane operator behind me. "You're happy when your pay's right at the end of the month and you can take things easy."

I was perspiring as I finished smoothing out a square meter. Then the Redhead came with a water bucket. He splashed the concrete with a brush and without a word took my float in his

9. *Junge Welt*, the daily newspaper of the Free German Youth organization.

[53]

hand. Nonchalantly he rubbed the crater-scarred surface smooth while holding a cigarette stub in the other hand and enjoying his last drag. With his forefinger he drew a number in the middle of the surface, wiped off the finger on his pants leg and called out, "Knolle, Bummi, cover it up!"

He turned his back to me and walked away.

I leaned against the ladder of the crane, exhausted. A voice yelled down, "Let the new one at a vibrator, otherwise she'll doze off."

v

I dreaded going to work more every day. I tried to console myself, thinking at least I wasn't going to freeze. Finally I talked myself into seeing the whole thing as a sporting event. While sitting in school rooms and university lecture halls, hadn't I longed for a real good workout?

So I started my training. In between vibrating, smoothing off, and making holes for the eyelets, I ran to get the shovel, scraped the mess from the forms together, and loaded it into the wheelbarrow. A job my fellow crew members tried to avoid.

When they took their smoke break behind the pile of concrete, I sorted stack wood.

The worst torture was at breakfast. Which way was I supposed to look?

I stared at my bread roll as though it were an open mystery novel.

Gradually my conditioning improved. After three weeks I could climb up on the high U-forms without a ladder and vibrate through four forms in a row.

There were fewer scornful looks from the others. They ignored me.

They seemed to be turning their attention more and more to the crane operator, the old jailbird from Berlin.

I caught myself listening to him.

Smoke break. I'm gathering up stack wood that's lying around.

"An' there was this other guy," the crane operator was saying, "a real oddball, Gimpy. Had a crooked leg, that's how he got the name. . . . He was gonna start up a combat unit.[10] Yak, yak, yak. About conscience and that stuff. And when the time comes and he thinks everybody's gonna come shufflin' up. . . . You're practicin' slow motion here, huh?" He looked down at me with a sneer. I was crouched next to Bummi, whose boot rested on the last piece of stray wood.

"Bummi, lift up your ballet slippers."

I carried the wood over to the stack, disappointed that I hadn't heard how things turned out for Gimpy.

One time I just about opened my mouth again.

Bummi had lifted the tarpaulin off a form that had been filled hours before, and when a cloud of dust rose up, he said: "Werner, look here, it's dry. If the concrete starts comin' on time now, we could pull the tarp from the mornin' job at noon and set up two shifts again. Then we'd get twice as much done every day. Think a'that, twice as much."

"Shut your trap," the Redhead snapped at him. "You wouldn't earn one mark more for it anyway."

Werner was silent.

Bummi didn't let up. "But at least take a look, it's dry. I think . . ."

"*You* don't do the thinkin' here," Werner responded angrily. "You follow my orders. I'll take care of *thinkin'* for ya."

I threw myself into my work. Provoked by Bummi's remark, Werner persisted with his sergeant's tone for two days. But his step became less certain, and the more he growled, the more he seemed to fear that he'd trip over his own feet when he passed by the forms filled with concrete.

I started to watch him.

Once, when the others were already in the canteen, he lifted

10. *Kampfgruppe*, an armed industrial militia group in the GDR. Under the control of the Communist party, such groups were supposedly for state defense.

up the tarpaulin from a slab poured that morning, rapped on the concrete with his knuckles and nodded.

At the lunch table, he poked around in his food before turning to Bummi. "You're right," he said in a low voice. "We could take the tarp off this morning's stuff already. But you know the others, and if the quota goes up . . ."

Bummi stared at him in disbelief.

My only consolation was the ten minutes each day that I sat on the john and read during the breakfast break. I had a Reclam paperback with me, the *Economical/Philosophical Manuscripts* by Marx, that I'd wanted to finish for a long time.

What I was reading stood in a strange relationship to what I saw everyday. What I saw consisted of construction site, eating, sleeping, earning money.

All around me hardly anything else was talked about.

I was on pay scale four, 750 marks a month, net. The things I could buy with that! A new stereo set, books, records, as many as I wanted to, a dress. . . . But when was I supposed to read the books, listen to the records? When could I wear the dress? More and more I felt indifferent, dull.

The others had done the same amount of work without me, sixteen forms a day. How had they benefited from my being there? More time to stand around, to smoke, and to listen to the crane operator.

VI

In recent weeks the concrete had arrived almost always in good time. And for several days now all the frost had been gone. When I set out in the morning, I could recognize roofs.

The Spree, black as india ink before, began to flow and to smell like a river. Some of the tugboats that passed by were freshly painted. There was a rustling and crackling in the air.

The workers who passed through the gate with me in the morning began to take on personalities. I became involved in conversations, snapped up bits of life histories. Tired passengers, riding the early morning tram in their jackets and parkas, spoke in a colorful way. Whoever began the day two hours later missed out on all of it.

"Here we go again, every day the same . . ."

"Yeah, older people are now the dumb-dumbs . . ."

"You can't really put it that way either, . . ." somebody responded. The rest of the sentence was swallowed up in the rattle of the tram.

I had to get out at the next stop. I forced my way past a young man in a stylish broad-brimmed hat.

"I'm gettin' out too," he said. He called me by my name, offered his hand, and introduced himself. "You don't know me anymore?" He took his hat off and patted it. "Yeah, I look different in this. I've got a job in the warehouse, drivin' the cargo carrier."

Now I recognized him, we'd often stood next to each other in front of the canteen.

"I'm in charge of rearrangin'," he said. "Makin' room for the new stuff. At least when my shift's over, I can tell what I've done. If I can't see that I go crazy. That's why I quit construction. My buddy says, 'You're crazy, they pay better here.' Doesn't matter, I said, I've gotta see what I've done. Just pokin' around with a shovel the whole day I go berzerk."

This conversation passed through my mind again as Knolle, while smoothing over a form, was saying, "This should really be like it was when we were kids, makin' pies in the sandbox. We had a good time . . ."

"Hm," said Joe, "what makes ya think a'that?"

"It was fun. And this . . . isn't really any different, only in size. . . . Why does somethin' that used t'be fun, now make ya wanna puke?"

"Well, then you were doin' it because ya wanted to, and now ya have to. Right?" Joe propped a hand on his rear and looked up at the sky.

The tall, brawny one was sitting on a pile of sidewalk forms nearby and cleaning hand floats. "Naw, Knolle," he said, "as a kid ya could see how things changed with every touch. The end re-sult was a pie or a castle. You could wonder at it: aha, I made that! But d'ya see the house that's gonna come outta these forms?"

The Redhead and the crane operator pulled a tarpaulin over the special form.

"When I think about where my best job was," the Redhead said, "I'll tell ya, it was when I was a LPG bricklayer[11] on the coast. We were buildin' pig sheds and plasterin' private homes on the side. When we left, the place was neat as a pin. . . . I coulda stayed right there. We earned good money too, but that wasn't the most important thing."

"That's bull," said the crane operator. "How much ya bring home affects your ol' lady's mood. The best job I had was when I was drivin' the diesel machine with the street cleaners. I had two boxes in back, one for coal that lasted me the whole winter, and the other for bottles. Money layin' in the streets, ya just needed t'bend over. Besides that I hauled some stuff for the flower guy and the vegetable guy. So plus my 400 wage I got another 400 marks. That was my best job."

"And why didn't ya keep doin' it?" asked Knolle.

"Well, I still was gettin' only 800. Had to teach swimmin' at the indoor pool on weekends so my old lady. . . . And ya can clear more here, . . . but with the diesel that time, I was poolin' my money together all by myself. Here ya jus' get it, even for doin' nothin'.'"

"In the village," the Redhead persisted, "the money almost didn't matter to me."

The crane operator laughed, the others laughed with him.

I was hoping that somebody would ask how things could be done differently here.

11. LPG, *Landwirtschaftliche Produktionsgenossenschaft* (Agricultural Pro-duction Cooperative). By the 1980s, agricultural cooperatives in the GDR controlled over 80 percent of the country's farmland and livestock.

My imagination started to work, the heavy vibrator seemed light in my hands.

VII

The next morning a snowstorm.

I raced back to my room, grabbed my ski sweater out of the closet, and put it on under my parka while running a marathon to the station. I caught the commuter train, but in Rummelsburg[12] the tram that was scheduled didn't come. The next one was full and wouldn't take on any more passengers. Half an hour late, I ran across the construction site. The tarpaulins over the forms were raised up like boils.

The crew had already changed clothes, all wore ski caps.

I said, "The tram . . ."

Werner looked at his watch. They left.

I changed my clothes. Since I didn't have a cap, I slapped on my helmet.

The cold bit into my ears. Under the hood of my parka I hadn't noticed how frigid it was.

Then the snow began to melt, gray slime fell from the sky.

"Slop," said Joe, as he examined the strands of hair that hung down to his chest.

Water dripped from my helmet.

We heaved the tarpaulins off the forms that we'd poured yesterday.

"I wonder where Baldy is," said Werner. "He's supposed t'pull out the slabs. Didn't he come with you on the tram?"

"No," someone answered. "Yesterday he wanted t'tie one on. I'm sure he's still sleepin'."

"If he doesn't come," said Werner, "I can't order any concrete."

We stood around for half an hour. The others smoked. I was rubbing my ears.

Joe yawned long and loud.

12. A station for the commuter train in the East Berlin borough of Lichtenberg.

"And where's the Retiree?"

"Reported in sick, has a cold."

"Tomorrow I'll be gone too," said Joe. "I'm givin' some blood."

"You get 45 marks and a day off. Says so on the bulletin board."

"Is it good for ya?" asked the Redhead.

"Yeah, my mother read in a magazine that it's suppose t'renew your blood."

"I'm comin' along," said Knolle.

"Well, then I'm givin' some too," said the Redhead. He was lisping more today than usual. "If I get a whole day off for it. Catch up on some sleep."

Werner exploded. "Are you guys crazy? If you're takin' time off, then each one on a separate day."

We stood around waiting and waiting.

An hour later the crane operator showed up. He was wearing a fur cap with the earflaps down. He had a lunch sack in his hand.

As Werner lectured him, he rolled his eyes and looked at the sky. When he turned to go inside to change his clothes, Werner yelled, "You climb up in that crane just the way you are!"

Werner ran over to the mixer. After the crane had pulled the first slab out of the form, we started lining them again.

Werner came back swearing. All the trucks were at the building site, there wouldn't be any coming before ten. That meant overtime. I had no feeling left in my toes.

"Head down!" Knolle gave me a shove and I ducked just as the heavy piece of concrete came whizzing by.

"Are you blind or somethin'?" yelled the crane operator. "If you don't watch it, I'll end up in jail."

The tall, brawny one pried the first empty forms apart with a crowbar. Joe went to give him a hand, scraping off the concrete that stuck in the joints like scabs. Rowing with his arms, Bummi stood up on a pile of slabs and gave signals to the crane operator. To the right, to the left . . . and released the crane hooks after a slab had found its place. The Redhead attached the hooks to the

[60]

fresh slabs. He swore steadily. A part of one eyelet had been set in too far for the hook to fit.

To console him, Werner said, "It'll work with three too." He looked up at the slab that hung crookedly in the air.

Werner waded through the sludge toward Knolle, who was standing next to me. "We'll start with the special slab," he said. He turned to me: "Oil it up."

I ran to the tool chest, surprised that my body could still move. I had felt numb all over. I took a pail, set it in front of the oil barrel, turned the barrel so that the stopper was above the pail, then with some effort unscrewed it. The oil sloshed out thick and black.

Then, after I had closed up the barrel and rolled it back, I got the broom and climbed with broom and pail into the first clean form. I dipped the broom into the oil and brushed it over the steel.

The work eventually warmed me up. I remembered a seventh grade physics class on the transformation of kinetic energy into heat and I worked faster. I was wishing I had a hundred such forms to lubricate.

But it only took me half an hour. Four times I'd had to fetch more oil. The last pail, still half full, I dragged back to the tool chest.

In the meantime the others had lined all the forms. There was nothing for me to do. We stood behind the pile of slabs and smoked. Though I was a smoker too, no one had offered me a light.

There was still an hour and a half until breakfast, and the concrete wouldn't arrive until after that.

"We'll be workin' overtime," said Werner. "You can thank him." He pointed at Baldy.

Baldy smoked his cigarette to the end and went to change clothes. Half an hour later he was back.

The heavy wet snow never stopped coming down.

[61]

I kept looking at my watch.

Somebody said, "Man, she's gotta watch on. The time'll never pass, take that thing off."

I stuck my watch in my jacket pocket, then I took it out and put it in my pants pocket. My work jacket was wet and getting heavier and heavier.

Knolle yawned, then they all yawned in turn.

I ran in place, counted the seconds and minutes. The others stood there like tin soldiers.

Finally Werner said: "Breakfast."

One hour later we were standing outside again, still no sign of concrete. After a glance at the office building, Werner ordered us to clean up the yard.

We scraped the slush into a pile, shoveled it into the wheelbar-rows, emptied them on the dumping grounds in back.

Finally the concrete came.

At home I lay in bed thinking I had died.

VIII

The next morning we stood around outside again.

It was snowing heavier than yesterday. The crane operator arrived on time, but the mixer had broken down and wouldn't be repaired before noon.

Werner stretched out his arms. "Let's get movin'. Clean up the trash."

I ran to get a scraper and scraped around in the snow.

The others didn't move.

"Everything's already been scraped up," said the Redhead.

"Then you guys just do it once more," said Werner gruffly. "Siedow looked down here yesterday, and if he sees that we're standin' around. . . . So let's go, get movin'."

The tall, brawny one turned slowly around in a circle like a tired dancing bear and stood still again.

I set my scraper aside.

[62]

"I'm sayin' don't stand around like sheep. There's gotta be trash somewhere!" Werner shouted.

"Get some concrete and you'll see how we move," said Joe calmly.

Werner changed his tune. "But you're gettin' paid for your time. . . . In the West you wouldn't get a cent . . ." Then giving in, he said, "Well, all right, but at least stand behind the pile."

All of us complied but Baldy, who pretended he hadn't heard anything.

It was no easier standing behind the pile than in front of it. What could I think about?

Going through world history in my mind, I chose a year: 1804. The French Revolution was over, Napoleon was emperor, the last of the Jacobins persecuted. . . . How did it go? My brain seemed frozen. I tried to calm myself. The others weren't poring over world problems either. Stand still and sleep.

As I started up from a drowse, I could no longer move my toes.

I looked over at Knolle, who stood there smoking. The cold didn't seem to bother him. He was getting paid for standing around.

I envied him and the others. Somehow I was the one ill-suited for life.

Now and then bits of conversation. "That was the goalie's fault. He shoulda jumped, thrown himself on the ball, but the way he was . . ." Joe demonstrated, his mouth pulled down disapprovingly. "That's how he stood there," he shouted, "like somebody was gonna come and tuck the ball under his arm."

I turned an ear in the direction of the mixer. Silence. "Anybody comin' along to Monte's today?" someone asked. "Ya missed somethin' yesterday, two guys really got into it."

"I'm comin'," said the Redhead. "Today for sure. Stand around the whole time and somethin' starts buildin' up. Maybe I'll find a guy to box with." He laughed, punched Joe in the side. "Well, should we have a go?"

[63]

When Joe raised his fists, Werner stepped between them. "Nothin' doin'! After work if ya want, that's fine."

Disappointed, the Redhead let his arms fall. Then he said: "That guy at the window with the dent in his forehead, . . . when I see him watchin' I go crazy . . ."

Another hour of silence.

I tried to give names to my moods, came up with seventeen synonyms, then miscounted when I wanted to put them in alphabetical order: "bitter," "depressive," "empty," "kiss-my-ass," "lethargic" . . .

"Looka that, he's got it good." Joe pointed up at the crane. "It's warm up there."

The crane operator stuck his head out of the cab, grinned. Then he held a pencil and a magazine out of the window and yelled, "Anybody know the name of the biggest river in India?"

To be sitting up there now seemed like paradise to me. The manager came slogging toward us, in rubber boots this time. He positioned himself in front of Werner and asked, half submissively, half patronizingly: "Could you assign someone to my office again?"

Without looking at him, Werner asked the others, "What you guys gonna do on Sunday?"

"Depends on the weather," said the tall one. "If it's nice, I go walkin' through Friedrichshain Park. They've got shish kebabs and curry sausage. . . . Sunday mornings I go drinkin' beer in Monte's. . . . And if it's like today, I'll stay in bed and read a mystery. Stop over if ya feel like it."

The manager was embarrassed. He shrugged his shoulders and tried again: "I need somebody to help with wage statements, drawing up lists."

And suddenly it happened. My arm went up, forefinger extended into the air as if I were a school kid. "Yes, I'll do it, I'll do it, Werner, if no one else wants to," I said.

Right afterward I wanted more than anything to dissolve into thin air. "Get movin'," Werner hissed.

[64]

He called out after us, "That's the last time, my friend. We're construction workers. Make your own lists."

Inside the manager's office, I sat down next to the radiator, enjoyed the warmth that flowed into me. I looked down at my boots. "Can I take them off?"

The manager nodded, took a pencil, paper, and a ruler from a drawer and set them out on the desk. I put my boots on top of the radiator and sat up at the desk in stocking feet.

There wasn't much to explain. I began to draw lines meticulously as if I were designing plans for a new city. I was happy. It seemed to me to be the best of professions, drawing up lists in the manager's quarters.

An hour later I didn't feel so good. I was ashamed of myself. I sat in the warmth inside, and the others? Why couldn't I endure what they endured?

Werner tramped in. "Have they finally got it fixed?"

The manager shrugged, pointed to the telephone. "Haven't called yet. That means no."

Werner grabbed for the receiver, dialed, then yelled: "What's goin' on? Have you? . . . What? We're standin' around freezin' our mitts. Deadheads!" He slammed the receiver down.

Without looking at me he left the room.

The manager busied himself with the radio, searching for a station. He chose a lively broadcaster, one with a Berlin accent reporting on an exhibition of purebred dogs: "A wild buying spree, so to speak. . . . First the man and then the dog, I always thought, but in this case it seems I'd better correct myself. . . . And not every dog suits a potential owner. For the man over there, for example, a fox terrier . . . no kidding, he's buying it. May I ask you, sir . . . but first of all our daily quiz question. Among the 20,000 dogs in Berlin, which breed carries off the prize? A tip: the Carelian Bear-dog isn't it. Now grab your pencils, our address: Berlin Radio . . ." The manager switched to a station playing rock music.

[65]

Sitting down across from me, he smiled.

I was not smiling.

"Have you been a manager long?" I asked, as disparagingly as I could.

"No, I'm still takin' the examinations. Use t'drive the 900 dump truck. Can't do that forever. The kids nowadays drive like wild animals. Ya get older. And then you're liable t'get rheumatism or a bad back. . . . Three years ago they selected me for the manager's training course." He tugged at his necktie.

Suddenly I felt sorry for him.

The door sprang open. A tall man with bloodshot eyes came lumbering in. "The mixer'll be ready in half an hour. Where's the trucks?"

"Well, at the building site. What are they supposed to . . . I've got them at the site."

"Get 'em over here!" The man leaned heavily on the desk and looked at the manager who was busy telephoning.

"Hello . . . What's happening with our trucks? We're gonna need 'em again ourselves. . . . The mixer is fixed and now . . . What? In the mud? That can't be. What'll we do now?" He looked at us helplessly and was just about to hang up when the tall man took the receiver out of his hand.

"What's goin' on? In the mud? But not all of 'em. That I'd like t'see. . . . Yeah, and send 'em over here right away! All four of 'em! Otherwise we'll send you guys. . . . Okay! And pull the other three out. Well, with the bulldozer, what else? No, *now!* We . . ." He listened a while intently, then bellowed, "Today, I say! Otherwise prefab parts over here has to shut down. What, already taken off? I don't give a shit, then you get on the bulldozer. Yeah, you! I'm sendin' another one over right away, then you've got half an hour t'get those things out. And if ya don't, this is the last time you're gettin' a vehicle from us."

The man put the receiver down calmly, yawned, walked with a heavy step to the door and let it close behind him.

"Ya don't learn that in training," said the manager with a sigh.

[66]

It wasn't so hard for me now to get up in the mornings. While still asleep I began the leap out of bed and was on my feet as soon as the alarm sounded. To trick myself, I'd set it so there would be only twenty minutes to catch the commuter train and if I wanted to be on time I had to function like a machine.

Once on the train, I woke up, rubbed my eyes, and finally could see. I fetched an apple and the sandwiches that I'd made the night before out of my bag. I chewed away, feeling fine until I thought of the previous day and the remarks that would probably be waiting for me now. It seemed as though I was heading for my execution.

We started lining the forms. The weather was different from yesterday. Warm wind and cold sleet, a kind of battle of the elements.

The concrete arrived before we had finished. The sides of the form loosened up with a groan under my crowbar. I forced them down with a kick, cleaned them off with a trowel.

When I was finished with the last form I ran up front to the first ones that were just being filled with concrete. While the others dug out the eyelet holes, I took up a hand float and began smoothing over the surface. The float didn't make nearly as many scratches as it had on the first days.

I was perspiring.

"Give it here," said Werner, not in an unfriendly way.

He took the float out of my hand. "You hafta press down a little with the front edge, not at all on the back one." He demonstrated.

I tried it. True enough, the cement surface looked as though it had been polished. And it required only half the effort.

"And now take a five-minute break," said Werner. "We don't need any dead bodies around here."

I thought I'd heard wrong.

Werner did the smoothing out while I sat down on the edge of the form.

[67]

Joe looked over, then Knolle, both without hostility it seemed to me.

The crane operator passed by and I was expecting a vile remark. He said nothing, he looked beyond me. What had happened?

"Toss the hammer over here," the Redhead called to me.

I lifted up the hammer. It was too heavy to throw, I carried it over.

"Thanks!"

He had thanked me. Then as we were rubbing down the special slab, Bummi said out of the blue: "That was great the time you didn't have no glasses for the schnapps and jus' started drinkin' outta the bottle. Nobody would thought you'd do it."

As I was shoveling the rest of the concrete into the wheelbarrow, the tall, brawny one took the shovel from me and said, "Careful, a yank like that and it'll all come down."

Like a fairy tale, I thought. I'm Miss Snow White.

I was finding the work easier.

It began snowing harder again. Werner informed us resignedly, "We have to work late. Orders from Siedow to catch up with the Plan.[13] . . . Actually not legal on such short notice. Should've . . . how long before?"

The others shrugged their shoulders.

"In any case it shoulda been announced a while in advance. We were at it late yesterday too."

"And *what* were we at?" Joe grumbled. "Standin' around because no one was operatin' the crane in Marzahn.[14] And I had a date. And today I'll miss it again," he said edgily.

"What d'ya want?" Werner asked. "You got somethin' extra for it." He rubbed the thumb and forefinger of his right hand together. "And today we're loadin' up."

13. Centralized economic planning in the GDR resulted in annual production goals, that is, plans, for combines, cooperatives, and factories.

14. An area in the borough of Lichtenberg.

The crane operator was satisfied. "Sure there was somethin' extra . . . long as we're gettin' paid I keep my yap shut."

"And what about the company?" I asked. "Does it mean a total loss?"

"So what," said the crane operator. "Last Sunday the guy drivin' crane in Unit Three had a taxi pick 'im up at home on the company's account. . . . I'm doin' it next time too. Without me you guys'd just be standin' around with your hands in your pockets."

"Yeah, but overtime has to be announced earlier," Joe persisted.

"Doesn't it say that in the workers' handbook?" I asked. I had paged through it in the manager's office yesterday.

"I'll go get it," said Werner. "Then we can go to the director . . ." He trudged out.

"If I stand her up again today," Joe said gloomily, "she'll dump me."

"You'll find a new one," said Knolle.

"Just try t'find one like her, one who doesn't start talkin' about gettin' married right away," said Joe. "And can she ever dance, a school teacher."

"School teacher?" the Redhead shook his head. "My ex was too. They can never shut up. I listened to a class of hers right after we got married. She was blamin' the capitalists for everything, even our juvenile delinquency. And the same thing at home. Only then I was the bad guy."

"Mine's different," said Joe. "Do ya think the handbook's gonna do any good?"

The crane operator responded calmly: "We had a guy with the street cleaners, too, who was always talkin' about the law. And you know where he ended up."

Werner came back, the book in hand, his finger stuck between two pages. He spread them open and read out the paragraph. Then he added, "I've got somethin' planned for today too. A court date for the divorce that my old lady has finally agreed to. And if I don't show up there . . ." Then turning to me, he asked: "But do ya think we can just go up to Wittmann? . . ."

"Goin' to Wittmann won't do no good," said Knolle. "You know that."

"Why not?" I asked.

"Wittmann is the director but Siedow gives the orders," said Werner hesitatingly. "Wittmann's worried more about the details, about safety regulations and each guy's problems, . . . but it all goes slow. Siedow's pace is hectic. He demands overtime, but he fulfills the Plan and you earn more. You're right, Knolle, we're better off goin' to Siedow."

He grasped my arm. "Are you comin' along?"

The two of us started walking.

Werner called back, "Take a noon break when you're finished. And if we aren't back before two, go ahead and change clothes."

It had stopped sleeting, the wind dried the air like pieces of clothing on a line.

x

We knocked, but Siedow's office was locked.

"Maybe they're having lunch," I said.

"They eat at twelve," said Werner, "and now it's quarter past one."

"Nobody's there," said a voice from behind us. It was the janitor. "Next time do a better job of wipin' your feet off."

A woman coming out of the adjoining office called back: "But I'll tell ya, Ursel, she'll be ridin' in Siedow's Volvo soon, eighteen, and with that snubby nose . . ." She noticed us and said, "They've all left, a meeting in the head office. What is it?"

I wanted to speak, but Werner nudged me. He said, "All right, we'll come back on Monday."

We turned around. The janitor called after us: "But with clean feet."

"We'd better keep workin'," said Werner indecisively. "We can't just. . . . Go ahead and eat, I've gotta call and cancel my court appointment. My wife won't mind, she'll be able to keep my checkbook a little longer."

I didn't say anything. Werner's face, I noticed, looked tired.

Ten minutes later he came into the canteen. "We'll keep pourin'," he ordered. "Siedow's not there and without him. . . . Where's Baldy?"

The others grinned.

"Took off," said the Redhead finally. "That's what you said . . ."

"Even so, he's got no business leavin'. Not even quittin' time yet." He poked around at his potatoes sullenly.

"We can't do no work without a crane operator. Who'll pull out the slabs?" Joe asked happily.

Werner slammed his knife and fork down so hard the gravy splattered.

"Aren't you gonna eat?" asked the tall one.

Werner shoved the plate toward him.

Though I had finished eating, I wasn't full and I looked enviously at the tall one, who was attacking Werner's cutlet.

"How come you're scrapin' around on an empty plate?" asked Knolle. "Get a second helpin'. We're the last ones, they gotta shove out what's left over. . . . Hey, Trude," he called out in the direction of the food counter, "what's in the pot? Bring it out here, your rabbits can eat grass."

A stout woman in her fifties approached slowly with a tray that held one dish of mixed vegetables and another of potatoes.

"There's still cutlets in the fryin' pan," said Joe. "I saw 'em. Get with it, Trude, otherwise we'll butcher you."

Laughter.

The woman brought in the cutlets.

Werner had propped his arms on the table and was massaging his forehead.

The tall one swallowed a huge bite and snickered. "In Monte's last night ol' Joe says to the whore, the red-headed one . . ." He glanced over at me, blushed, then went on. "He says to her, 'You look like a eunuch.' She asks, 'What's that suppose t'be?' And Joe says, 'Oh, somethin' refined, an Egyptian queen.'" He gave Joe a poke. "Right?" Joe nodded and grinned.

The tall one slapped his thigh. "And then the way she strutted around. Like this." He stood up and demonstrated.

"What's a eunuch?" asked Bummi. "That don't click with me."

"Ya, what is it, anyway?" the lady in the kitchen called out.

The tall one busied himself with the rest of his cutlet.

After a while Joe said, "I just heard some guy sayin' it to a dame over on Prenzlauer Avenue. Well, in any case, somethin' disgustin' out of old Egypt."

"Eunuchs are castrated men," I said. "They were government officials or harem guards. And because they'd been castrated, they got very fat."

Fresh laughter.

The tall one looked over at me respectfully. "The things you know."

"I'm fed up with whores," the Redhead said. "I wanna real girlfriend again."

"You think I'm not sick of 'em?" another one asked. "But what ya gonna do? The nice girls . . . barely go dancin' with one and right away it's over to Mama and Papa's for coffee, then comes the question, 'Well, when are you getting engaged?' It gets ya fed up in a hurry."

"So that leaves only whores," said another, "unless ya wanna start settin' up a household right away again. And this way ya can spend as many nights in Monte's as ya please."

"But that's only in Berlin," said Joe. "In the little Podunk I come from ya can't get divorced because of the neighbors. And there's no whores either, at any rate ya don't know where to find 'em."

"Yeah, Berlin," said the tall one, "here ya can try out a few things."

"There's really a lot that's different here," said Knolle. "When I first got here, the company gives me the key to my room, Wins

Street, three floors up. I rang the bell. Nobody answered. 'On vacation,' says the neighbor lady. I unlock the door, find a note on the coatrack: 'Welcome to our house,' it says. 'Your room is down the hall and to the right. Please water the flowers in the living room.' They didn't even know what kinda guy I was. . . . Where I come from, if somebody has a painter comin' in, they take a day off work to watch 'im. Keep 'im from stealin' anything."

The talk shifted between rooms, landlords, and workers' dormitories until the last one had finished his cigarette.

An hour later, after we'd showered and changed and were passing by the doorman on the way to the street, Knolle said, "We'll be in Monte's tonight, that's . . ."

The Redhead told me the names of two intersecting streets in the district of Prenzlauer Berg.[15] "If you're not doin' anything, come over. Where d'ya live? . . . Ya take number 71 to the church and go right at the next corner."

Knolle added, "Yesterday we were talkin' about ya. In your place we woulda quit by now. Every one of us."

At home I stood in my room a while without moving. Then I dug around in my records and put on the Beatles. I opened a bottle of expensive red wine that I'd been saving two years for a special occasion. I drank to this strange day. A pity that I couldn't toast with anyone.

When the bottle was empty, I danced through the room and swore at myself, the naive one.

I slept for two hours, washed up, and put on my best skirt and my best blouse.

While sitting down to supper I thought, it isn't that easy to wear down humankind.

15. Prenzlauer Berg is an old working-class neighborhood in East Berlin.

Philemon and Baucis

·

Beginning of September. In the courtyard behind my apartment building the garbage simmering in the trash containers sends out an odor of rotten fish.

One morning, a little after five, I start up out of a dream. It occurs to me that it's Saturday.

Fifteen minutes later I'm off on my bicycle. I take it along in the subway, get out at the end station. I pedal through the woods.

Then I reach the water. Here there's even a bit of wind. It sails into a tall maple tree, tears out a clump of yellow leaves. Slowly they flutter down on me.

I change out of my clothes, swim in a wide circle.

When I ride on, I'm calm and relaxed.

In front of me the path suddenly stops. I jam my foot on the brake.

I see the arm of a river, a pier stretching far out. But no trace of a ferry.

Behind me, to the left, are many trees and bushes. A path leads off to the right. Laths, colorfully painted, are shimmering behind three stately linden trees.

I hear chickens cackling. Lean my bike against the railing of the pier and follow the worn path.

In front of me is a summerhouse like a boat, or maybe not a boat? Patched up with wooden laths of all colors.

On the green door an old railroad sign: *No Entrance* in curlicue letters. Next to it a nesting box. On the other side, hanging from a cord, a pot of geraniums in bloom.

The front yard is covered by an awning made of colored strips of canvas sewn together. Beneath it, between a small bench and a chair that's been painted blue: a round table with an oilcloth covering, two beer and two schnapps glasses, a bill for the radio,[1] a box of *Riesaer Matches*, an overflowing ashtray, a knife sharpener, and a package of *Real Cigarettes*. In the middle, holding a big bouquet of asters as varied in color as the summerhouse, is a coffeepot with blue polka dots, minus its spout.

Next to the summerhouse, a flower bed with chives and parsley.

The thin voice of a church bell comes across the water and wraps the entire scene in an aura of peacefulness.

Who lives here anyway? I asked myself.

A rooster so gaudy he could be out of a picture book walks up slowly, stops in front of me and looks me over from head to foot with his big round eyes.

The door of the house creaks open. An old woman in wooden clogs, wearing a checkered wraparound apron, takes a step outside. She squints into the sun, then yawns and stretches, making sure not to spill anything from the large coffee mug in her right hand.

"Hello there," she says to the rooster.

He answers with a loud greeting.

"Good morning," I say.

While carefully setting the coffee mug down on the table, she asks in a throaty voice, "What are you looking for?"

I point to the opposite shore.

"The ferry doesn't go until nine-thirty," she says. Then clears off the table and disappears. She comes back with a very big loaf of bread under her arm, a slab of butter in one hand, and a second coffee mug in the other. She clumps in and out a few more times,

1. A license fee.

[75]

each time taking the trouble to bend her knees in front of the table and slurp coffee from her mug.

Finally the table is set for breakfast.

The old woman stoops over, props one hand on the small bench and sits down. She calls toward the house: "Fritze, where are you?" Then clamps the bread in front of her breast and starts hacking off thick slices. After she's called out "Fritze" once more, and "Your coffee's gettin' cold!" the door opens.

An old man appears in faded blue cotton trousers, his tanned upper body is bare. Slightly bent, he drags one leg. Deliberately, as if in slow motion, he sits down on the chair opposite the old woman. He lifts the mug in both hands, begins to slurp.

The woman spreads thick layers of butter and marmalade on a slice of bread and reaches it across to him. "Eat, Fritze."

Then she glances over at me. "Ah, you're still here. . . . Fritze, she wants t'take the ferry across. I tol' her it's too early. . . . Well, sit down with us. Wanna cup a'coffee? But it's only artificial stuff."

Even before I nod, she's swaying toward the summerhouse. She returns with a third coffee mug, sets it on the table and slides over on the bench invitingly.

The mug is so full that I have to slurp at first. The old woman looks me over quickly, then says, "You're not from Berlin, right?" I shake my head.

She is satisfied, hands me a freshly buttered slice of bread.

"Here, eat somethin'. Or would ya rather have the crust?"

Thanking her, I take the bread and start eating. Then I say, "Your summerhouse has an unusual shape."

"Was a shootin' gallery before," the old woman explains with her mouth full. "Twenty-five years ago there was an amusement park here."

She's already buttering the next slice, and breaks off a piece for a ruffled sparrow that walks toward her on the table. "Here, my dear," she says.

I look at the two old people.

Both are tall and lean, muscular as rowers, their tanned faces good-natured and calm. Their hands are worn.

He is baldheaded. She has a thin, whitish-gray braid going down the back of her neck like a mouse's tail.

While she eats her breakfast heartily, he nibbles on the bread as if he had poorly fitting dentures.

The woman watches the man worriedly.

"And where do you live during the winter?" I ask.

"During the winter? Then we live in the city. Prenzlauer Berg,[2] if you've ever heard of it. It's no place t'live." She gestures contemptuously with her hand. "From our window all ya can see is beams, plaster, bricks, an' iron. Nothin' but dirt. For the last forty years."

She spits, draws a cigarette out of the package, clamps it between her lips. "But we've had this place for twenty-five years. Set up a fishin' association."

She points behind the house. "Others over there. Retired like us. My husband got it all goin'." She nods respectfully. "Ol' Fritze, I never woulda thought it'd work out. . . . Come, eat, my dear. You're still nibblin' on the first piece. . . . But now we hafta clear outta here." With a forceful puff she exhales the cigarette smoke.

"Or maybe you wanna go fishin'?" she asks the man. "Go ahead, Fritze, see if anything's bitin'."

The old man does not stir. Finally he lays the bread aside, takes the mug in both hands and slurps with a sound that has something in it of exhaustion, resignation.

"Why is that?" I ask.

"Everythin' here's gonna be torn down," she replies gruffly. "Gonna be a chicken farm put up. Then this here'll be only mud and chicken turds."

She gestures in an upward direction by lifting her head. "Well, it's not really *woods* here but still better'n Prenzlauer Berg. That's why we don't wanna leave. Everything's different here. Even the

2. A run-down working-class quarter of East Berlin.

people . . ." Again she points behind the house. "Fritze couldn't have set up any association in the city with these folks, huh Fritze?"

She's quiet for a while.

"But that's not possible," I say. "They can't just . . ."

"Oh, yes they can." She shrugs her shoulders. "We've been all over tryin' t'do somethin' about it, huh Fritze? Said we didn't want any money, we just wanna move to another place, somewhere on the water. We'd put together another place. But nothin'!" She spits again.

In an increasingly roundabout way she reports every undertaking in the matter, as if what she says is beyond her comprehension. Until suddenly she breaks off in mid-sentence and concludes: "When nothin' did any good, we thought we'd try the federal government.[3] But not a chance. We were at it one whole day, huh Fritze? Go to this room, and go to that room. . . . Finally we wore out. It seemed like we were always goin' in a circle. No, all that don't do no good. Now we just hafta make the best of it."

The old man rubs his hand slowly over his white beard stubble, meanwhile staring at the oilcloth on the table.

The woman nervously reaches a cigarette toward him. "Here, Fritze, have a smoke." He doesn't move.

I tell them they should nevertheless file a petition.

"Somethin' in writing?" asks the woman. "You think that'll help?" Then she shakes her head again. "I'm makin' the best of it. Just that Fritze. . . . Why don't ya go fishin', my dear."

We are silent.

I look over at the colorful laths.

The old woman notices, smiles and says, "Ya, you can tell this was a shootin' gallery at one time. We bought it twenty-five years ago and jus' covered it over, huh Fritze?"

3. Staatsrat (Council of State), a collective body formally elected by the Volkskammer (Peoples' Chamber) composed of a chairman, in this case Erich Honecker, seven vice-chairmen, members, and a secretary.

The church bell rings again. The old woman raises her head and says, "You have t'be goin', otherwise you'll miss the ferry."

On the water I take a place at the stern.

The two old people sitting at the table grow smaller and smaller.

Then I can make out only the three linden trees.[4]

---

4. According to Ovid's account of Philemon and Baucis, the visiting gods rewarded the elderly couple for their hospitality by transforming their humble cottage into a marble temple. Philemon and Baucis's wish to die at the same time was eventually granted and their bodies were changed into trees, a linden and an oak.

Feldberg and Back

·

It was Sunday. Cornelia's boyfriend had called. Instead of going riding with her in the countryside he wanted to watch soccer. If she felt like it, she should come over.

She didn't feel like it, she wanted to be outside.

She had just finished her *Abitur* examinations,[1] but she wasn't happy about it. The cramming and the fretting had exhausted her.

She wanted to get out of Berlin, but where to?

Her mother was at a health spa, her father in Moscow on a business trip.[2] Except on the telephone, she hadn't talked to anyone for two days.

She called Sabine's, nobody answered.

Surely they were in Mecklenburg,[3] working on their cottage. She looked out the window. It was cool and rainy outside, but she wanted to get away from the city. She checked the train schedule. The train to Neubrandenburg via Prenzlau[4] had just left.

It occurred to her that others her age often hitchhiked. Was she too scared to do it, or too well brought up? She pictured her

1. Comprehensive oral and written examinations usually coming at the end of the two-year advanced secondary school in the GDR. Before entering a university, prospective students were required to pass the *Abitur*.

2. An indication that Cornelia's father is among the privileged elite in GDR society.

3. An area of many small lakes near Berlin.

4. Cities located north of Berlin in the *Bezirk* Neubrandenburg.

[80]

father's face if he were to see her on the roadside from his company car.

She looked at the city map to find out which tram went to the highway and walked out of the apartment.

In the elevator it crossed her mind that she should really take a warmer jacket or her raincoat along. She was too lazy to turn around. Besides it was July.

She sat in the nearly empty 49 tram for over half an hour. Finally she stood on the roadside, hand outstretched.

There was little traffic, no trucks, and in the cars were married couples, some with children, some without. Many drivers indicated by their looks and gestures that they would like to take her along, but . . . they glanced at the seat beside them and shrugged their shoulders. Obviously the weekend was no time for hitchhiking.

She was planning to turn back when a vw with West Berlin plates stopped beside her.

"Why did you take your hand down?" the driver asked through the open window. "Don't you want to go toward Prenzlau?"

While getting in she said, "I just took an examination in civics. When you see a West license, you think: enemy of the working class."[5]

Surprised, the man looked her over as he started off, stopped, and said: "Then you'd better get out. I don't want to get you into trouble."

"No, no," she said. "Go on."

He told her his name and said he was a doctor.

She introduced herself. Just graduated from advanced secondary school, beginning September she'd be at a university studying law. But now it was time for vacation. In two weeks she'd be going with her parents, her boyfriend, and his parents to a company vacation lodge in Ahrenshoop.[6]

5. *Klassenfeind.*
6. A town on the Baltic Sea.

The driver said he had traveled halfway around the world and recently asked a friend which places were still worth visiting. He'd said, "In the GDR there are some really charming spots, Feldberg[7] for example . . ."

He showed her on the map *Feldberg and Surrounding Area* the walking route that he had traced for himself.

"By midnight," he said, "I have to be back at the border crossing.[8] And where do you want to go?"

She named a village that she thought must be near the highway.

He looked in the Road Atlas that had been lying open on the backseat. "Then you'll have to get out in D.[9] And how will you go from there?"

"From D. it's only six kilometers, I'll walk those."

"I'll drive you there. That's not far out of the way."

The man was in his early forties, tall and lean. He had thinning hair like her father and in general resembled him. That calmed her.

She looked out the window at the brown pasture, a few rays of sun came through the clouds.

"Can you open the roof?" she asked.

"Okay," he said.

He opened the car roof. The stream of air was pleasant. She wanted to tell him, but remained quiet.

Now they were passing a long strip of meadow with yarrow, thyme, St. John's wort. The meadow seemed unreal to her in this gloomy summer.

For something to do she was rummaging in her bag and happened to lay aside a book from Insel Press.

"Do you like to read?" the man asked.

7. A small city located directly north of Berlin in the *Bezirk* Neubrandenburg.

8. The speaker, a resident of West Berlin, has a GDR tourist visa for one day only.

9. An abbreviation in the original text.

She nodded. "This is one of yours. Böll. Are you familiar with the *Irish Diary*?"[10] Amused, he laughed. "Have you come to the place yet where the boy is in the tavern and pours a few too many drops of vinegar on the potato chips and the landlady runs after him screaming, 'You scoundrel, do you want to ruin me?'"

"I read that last night. A ragged-looking man gives her ten shillings so she'll let the boy off."

He smiled and said, "I think the next sentence is the most important one in the entire book: 'Whoever lives poetry instead of writing it pays 10,000 percent interest.'"

She didn't realize how long she would be puzzling over this sentence.

They exchanged reading suggestions. He recommended Latin Americans to her: Márquez, Asturias, Fuentes, Rulfo. For him she named Trifonov, Aitmatov, Shuksin.

He stopped the car, got a notebook out of his jacket pocket and wrote down the names.

Then they were already at the turnoff leading to the village where she wanted to go.

"That really went fast," she said.

"Is anyone expecting you?"

"Not really, I wanted to visit some friends. I was going stir crazy in Berlin."

"Why don't you come along to Feldberg if you've never been there? Things go better if there's someone to talk to."

She intended to get out, but surprised herself by saying, "All right," and remained seated.

They reached Feldberg around noon. She was hungry and asked, "Want to get something to eat?"

"Okay."

They tried three different restaurants, but everything was

10. Heinrich Böll (1917–85), author of *Irisches Tagebuch*, 1957. In the GDR the Insel Press of Leipzig was known for publishing international literature of high quality.

[83]

filled up with FDGB vacationers.[11] The fourth was closed. From the trunk of his car the man brought out French cheese and a box of pretzels. They ate, it tasted good. Then they looked at the map and started out walking.

He asked about her childhood.

There wasn't much to tell: Berlin, the apartment house next to Friedrichshain where she'd gone sledding or played soccer. Since her parents were often on business trips, she was home alone a lot. She got bored, then she started reading and painting. Painting was her hobby. She attended a drawing club in the district's *Kulturhaus.*[12]

"And how were things with you?" she asked.

His father was a soldier, killed in '43. After the war he and his mother walked from East Prussia to Berlin, then they lived a long time in a rear-court apartment building in Wedding.[13]

"That's how I became a Berlin resident," he concluded.

Cornelia corrected him: "*West* Berlin resident."

He laughed, said something that included the word *Wall.*

She corrected him: "*national border.*"[14]

When he again laughed, she explained at length why it was necessarily called the national border.

She talked and talked as she had during her oral examination the day before yesterday. The man did not interrupt. Suddenly it

---

11. FDGB, Freier Deutscher Gewerkschaftsbund (The Confederation of Free German Trade Unions). The largest labor organization in East Germany, FDGB provided a holiday service for its members, including partially subsidized vacations and package trips for families.

12. *Kulturhaus*: a state-sponsored cultural center. See note 2 of "The Tall Girl."

13. Formerly a province in the northeast of Germany, East Prussia is now divided between Poland and the Soviet Union. Wedding is a borough of West Berlin.

14. According to the Communist government in East Germany, the Berlin Wall was erected as a protective border against the imperialistic threat emanating from the West. Cornelia has obviously been influenced by this line of thinking.

seemed to her as if she had paper in her mouth, but she continued speaking and waited nervously for the man to object. She wanted to argue with him.

The man remained silent. He looked at her pensively. Then he stopped walking and said, "Where are we anyway?"

They were on a path. There was no sign of the lake they were looking for. A boy came by walking a horse, and they asked him the way. It turned out they had gone in the wrong direction.

"Let's drop the subject," the man said accommodatingly. "Otherwise we'll never get to the lake."

They arrived at Small Luzin and stopped in at the restaurant on the shore. After trying in vain to get tea, cider, or even lemonade, they ordered coffee.

Three times the waitress had to say, "We only have coffee," before the man believed it. "Coffee and cheesecake."

While they were eating cheesecake, he conversed with vacationers from Gera.[15] He wanted to know what they did on days like this when the weather was unfit for swimming.

He was taken aback by the answer: "There's a television in the lodge and we come over here to drink coffee twice a day."

On the path again, he told about his hiking with tent and backpack, described meals, landscapes and people, and repeated conversations that had impressed him.

To their left, between thick beech trunks, lay the lake: dark green, calm and cool, with only a single rowboat. On the opposite shore a dense woods stretched up the slope. They were met by an older married couple, both with canes. Her companion greeted them and asked for directions. The couple explained in considerable detail.

When they had gone on, Cornelia said, "But we already knew that."

He smiled. "It's nice the way one gets information here. The

15. The major city in the *Bezirk* Gera, in the southern part of the GDR.

people in general are friendlier. Last year, in Thuringia,[16] I noticed the same thing."

"Then come live on this side," she said tauntingly.

After a while he said, "Why not? As a doctor here at the Charité[17] . . . but I like to travel. I still want to go to Ireland, South America, everywhere."

"And that's all?" she asked. "Otherwise you think this is paradise?"

"What's paradise," he said calmly. "As far as I know it doesn't exist anywhere. At least here an ex-Nazi wouldn't come in during my counseling hours and give me hell because I refuse to treat him. Would you like to hear something like that?"

For some reason she became angry and suddenly started talking about her four years at the advanced secondary school, all sorts of stories about teachers and students. "If you've expressed your opinion three times without results, the fourth time you forget about it," she said. "And then how much of yourself have you got left? Just don't make trouble, always be careful who you're saying something to. You think that's good too?"

The man turned around and looked at her. She stopped short.

"What is it? I'm listening to you."

She was suddenly ashamed of herself. Did she have to tell a totally strange man from the West what she held back from her parents and her boyfriend? She, an honors graduate, winner of the Herder Medal?[18] She, who was to have her university education paid for?[19]

16. A region in the southwestern part of the GDR between the Werra and Weisse Elster rivers.

17. Historically famous as a hospital and medical research center, located in East Berlin.

18. Awarded for academic excellence at the level of the GDR advanced secondary school.

19. Education at colleges and universities in the GDR was fully subsidized by the state.

And if he happened to be a journalist and her wailing showed up next week in the *Spiegel?*[20]

She stopped and wanted to turn around.

The man walked on slowly.

Hesitating, she followed him.

For a long time they walked in silence.

Then a surprising view opened up to them.

Beyond the lake a sandy slope. The sun, having made its way through the cloud cover, turned it the color of ocher.

Reddish roofs in the background.

The man turned toward her. "Do you see?"

He seemed cheerful and relaxed, his face was almost handsome. She regretted her suspicion. Finally she said: "If you were in my place, would you think everything was good then too?"

She swallowed and looked at her feet.

The man waited until she caught up to him, put his arm around her shoulders and shook her lightly. "They are serious matters," he said. "In the West anyone can talk openly about the kinds of things that anger you. Nothing happens to them, nobody listens anyway. At least punishments show that you've reached somebody."

He waited for her reply and then went on. "In the West you need all of your strength to keep from becoming totally insensitive or materialistic. Scylla and Charybdis, are you familiar with the *Odyssey?* He stopped in the middle of his sentence and pointed at a raspberry bush with large red berries.

She asked if they could rest.

Again he said, "Okay."

She ate without tasting much. In her mind she repeated his words, turned and twisted them, nodded suddenly and, as she had done as a child, looked up at the sky with an open mouth.

The man stepped behind her, said, "Hold your mouth open," and fed her with a handful of raspberries. "Should we become friends?" he asked. "My name is Armin."

20. The major weekly news magazine in West Germany.

She nodded and told him her first name.

They walked slowly, and arrived at a place called Carwitz.

Clean little houses, gardens in which women were clearing weeds or picking berries.

In front of the village cinema young people on motorcycles and mopeds were gathered, speaking the jargon of the billboard advertising a movie, something about "Kill Me . . ."

"Our trash goes around the world," Armin said.

Then he greeted another married couple who approached them in short leather pants, striped knee stockings, and Tyrolean hats. He asked the way to the top of Captain's Mountain.

The man described it in broad Saxon,[21] the woman nodded at each word and added, "But no captain's sittin' up 'ere."

"Oh," Armin said, "you're from Vogtland?"[22] He thanked them before the delighted woman could answer.

As they passed the village tavern, Cornelia said, "Maybe they'll have hotdogs or soup."

"Okay," he said. "Let's go in."

There weren't any hotdogs, instead so-called pork sausages with lots of mustard, and beer that quenched their thirst.

It had rained outside in the meantime. The sun shone as they started climbing Captain's Mountain.

"Well," said Armin, "isn't this a bit of paradise? One doesn't have to go hiking across Malaysia with a backpack."

He read aloud from the plaque that was nailed on a tree: " 'Grave Mound from the Bronze Age.' . . . Somehow you feel that the old Teutons were already here," he said. "Two thousand years, always the same game: love, war, death . . ."

She stood on the peak of the hill, rowed in the air with her arms and had the notion that if she wanted to fly away now she

21. *Sächsisch*, a German dialect spoken in Saxony, a region in the southeast part of the GDR that includes the cities Leipzig, Dresden, and Karl-Marx-Stadt (Chemnitz).

22. A mountainous area in the southeastern part of the GDR. The doctor correctly links the couple's dialect with Vogtland.

could. She felt free. The last three kilometers, uphill and downhill back to the Small Luzin, took them two hours.

They examined the gorse that had been frozen during the last winter, but at the foot of one decrepit bush she found a spot of fresh greenery.

Armin was delighted by it. Suddenly she was shocked by how much she liked him.

From a lookout post at the edge of the woods they gazed across the lakes, across the hills with alfalfa fields, and suddenly he was talking about the street in Kreuzberg[23] where he lived.

West Berlin, said Cornelia, didn't exist in her imagination. For her the world came to an end at the Brandenburg Gate.

Armin didn't want to believe her. There was, after all, television.

"At home we don't watch West television."

Wasn't she interested, he asked, in what was on the other side of the Wall.

"What for? What I don't know can't hurt me."

"Isn't that too easy?"

She called him several names, then burst into tears.

"You'll fall down in a second," he said and drew her closer to himself.

She yanked her arm free, slid over to the ladder and climbed down.

She started walking without looking back.

A quarter of an hour later he caught up with her. He began chatting cheerfully, as if nothing had happened.

It was dark, she was cold.

He gave her his jacket and helped her put it on.

When they reached the lake shore the ferry was no longer in operation. He was shocked when he looked at his watch.

"I'm afraid we'll have to swim," he said.

23. A borough of West Berlin with low-rent areas that have attracted students, foreign workers, artists, and young political activists.

A couple was sitting on the pier in front of them. The boy turned around and said, "In this cold, you're crazy!"

"We have to be in Berlin by twelve," said Armin. "My car is in Feldberg."

The boy stood up and checked the rowboats rocking in the water on both sides of the pier.

"A pity," he said. "All of them are chained up."

"Then we'll swim over," said Cornelia.

"You think you can make it?"

"I'll come along," said the boy. "I'll carry your girlfriend's things over."

He started taking off his clothes. Armin was faster and was already in the water.

She removed her clothes. The girl helped her roll her things together into a bundle that her boyfriend could grip in one hand.

She got into the water, swam, and soon she felt warmth and contentment. As they approached the other shore, she was almost disappointed.

Armin gave her his jacket for drying off.

They thanked the boy, who said: "Have a good trip home."

They watched him while they dressed and waited until he was on the opposite shore.

They ran a marathon race to the car.

Once inside, she felt warm. Again they ate pretzels and cheese.

Then she grew tired. He said, "Open your mouth," and fed her the last piece of cheese. His hand touched her lips for a moment, he brushed a strand of hair away from her forehead. She looked away quickly.

For the return trip they took the expressway on the other side of Prenzlau.

She leaned back, the warm air streamed from the heater.

After a while he asked, "What are you thinking about?"

She had thought about how natural and uninhibited his movements were in contrast to the cramped way she walked, talked, and laughed, exactly like her parents, her boyfriend, his parents.

She didn't answer.

He changed the subject, spoke of a film comedy that he'd seen recently and imitated the leading man. It seemed to please him when he made her laugh.

He lay his hand on her shoulder, looked at her with a smile and said, "It's a pity we're getting back so late."

"Why?" she asked.

"Because I'd like to sleep with you."

She caught her breath and swallowed.

"You're not saying anything. Isn't that what you want too?"

"Yes, only no one's ever said that to me so directly before and without having poured two bottles of wine down me first."

"Seriously?" he asked, surprised.

She nodded, then she had to laugh.

"You wouldn't believe," she said, "how funny many people are. As if they were afraid of themselves. I'm that way too. But you're not going to ask about my boyfriend?"

"No," he said. "You're not in love."

"How do you know that?"

"I just think so." He touched her hand. "Were you ever really in love?"

She wanted to say yes, but hesitated.

"Probably not," she said, "not with my boyfriend and not with the one I had before."

"And now?" he asked.

"Now probably," she said softly and was happy that it was dark.

"But I could be your father."

"Even so," she said. "Do you have some kind of hobby?"

He shook from laughing. "Only you could ask something like that now. . . . Skydiving. I'm sure you'd like it too."

They were driving 150 kilometers an hour.

Then the city appeared. She saw the familiar streets, buildings, slogans. Suddenly she noticed how her heart was beating.

What was she getting herself into? With *a man from West Berlin*. She heard her parents and her school teacher pronounce the words. Then they were at the border crossing.

"We still have ten minutes. Should we get out?" he asked.

Silently they walked up and down the sidewalk. Then he stopped and turned her face toward him.

"Look at me," he said. He stroked her cheeks, her eyebrows, and lips with his fingertips. His tanned face was pale.

"Tomorrow I'll come for you right after work, all right?"

He asked for her address, she answered without looking at him.

Then it was twelve o'clock. He took her head in his hands and kissed her. As he drove away, he waved through the open roof of the car. She couldn't fall asleep. She took a sleeping pill. In three hours she was awake again, sat down at her father's writing desk and tried to draw: clouds, the frozen gorse bush with a spot of green at its base, Armin's profile.

Toward morning she grew tired, she lay down and slept.

She got up, yanked slacks, sweaters, and a skirt out of her closet, tried them all on in front of the mirror and found that nothing was suitable. She had the faded jeans from yesterday on again when the doorbell rang. She rushed to the door, pulled him inside, they embraced. Then they went hiking through Ireland with backpacks, it rained, because it always rains there, they laughed about it and argued over how much interest you have to pay when you live poetry instead of writing it . . .

About three in the afternoon she awoke, cleaned up her room, even vacuumed the carpet, dusted. Then she put on a piano concerto by Schumann. She turned the volume knob as high as it went. She showered, dressed, sat down on the couch and rested her head on her knees.

An hour later she felt hungry. She spread butter on a slice of bread, gagged hopelessly on the first bite and threw the bread into the garbage pail.

She put the record on for the fourth time. From the next-door apartment came the voice of the TV newscaster announcing the evening's program.

Suddenly she was crying. The doorbell would never ring.

She had given him a phony address.

A Week in Berlin

.

"I'm anxious to see what all there is."

"What?" Emmi pokes her small freckled nose out of the corner next to the window where she's dozed off.

"I'm anxious to see what's in the shops," Lucie repeats. She glances at the dainty watch suspended from a gold chain around her neck. "Aren't we almost there?"

"Yes," says Emmi, now fully awake. She straightens the short sleeves of her white blouse, sits up a little, smoothing out her skirt, and lays her hands in her lap expectantly. She smiles at her friend. "How I've looked forward to this trip. My first time in Berlin."

Emmi is still working. Her company, a spinning mill, has sublet a small apartment in Berlin and made it available to employees during the summer.

Since Emmi didn't want to travel alone, she invited Lucie, an old classmate from school, to accompany her.

Ever since her marriage forty years ago, which made her the richest woman in the village, Lucie tended to look down on Emmi. But Lucie is lonely now, and with Emmi willing to lend a sympathetic ear to her complaints, the friendship has been renewed.

It is the end of August.

Lucie is perspiring and fans herself with a magazine. Her broad, suntanned face reveals the beginnings of a mustache.

Gasping for breath, she blurts out: "Oh, what do I need! I've got everything, my closets are overflowing."

"Then why did you bring so much money along?"

Lucie gives a start, glances about the empty compartment suspiciously. Moves a hand over to protect her purse.

Then she says, "Well, it needs to be spent. I don't have children. Is the government suppose t'inherit it? And after all, we want to have something from Berlin."

"Yes," says Emmi, "I'd really like to go to the opera. Once in your life, I think, you have to have been to the opera."

"Whatever for? I was at the opera with Bruno once. Forty years ago, we were engaged at the time. Such garbage! Some guy sings, 'Oh, you are so delicate and frail,' and a fat lady comes out. And apart from that you can hardly understand a thing. The whole time I was thinking: I hope she dies soon."

"And I made sure to bring my good dress along."

"I packed my good things too. Some evening we'll go to an expensive place where the waiters'll be in tails and serve us somethin' fancy. And maybe there'll be dancing too."

"Dancing? You think somebody'll still dance with us?"

"Why not? There are widowers our age too. And could be . . ." Lucie winks, "could be one'll even feel like moving to the Thuringian Forest."[1]

"Yes, with you maybe," Emmi says softly. "You've got a house and money." She smiles. "Maybe I'll find a pretty ring."

She looks down at her small, worn left hand, dreamily runs the forefinger of her right hand up and down her ring finger. "I never had one. Always spent everything on my grandsons. But I promised myself I'd buy a ring with my first pension money."

Lucie stretches her hands out. "A pity I've got enough rings, otherwise I'd buy one too. But there's no more room, see?"

Emmi glances shyly at the hands in front of her nose.

"They're beautiful," she says, "but a small one with a cheap stone is enough for me."

---

1. A wooded mountain range in the southwestern part of the GDR.

"Nonsense, if it's going to be a ring, then a diamond. All these came from Bruno. Ah well . . ." She sighs. "Yesterday I was at the cemetery again, it's already more than a year since he's been gone."

A tear rolls slowly down to her chin. Lucie wipes it away. "I'm anxious to see what kind of apartment it is," she says. "Belongs to a doctor, you say?"

"Yes, but not a doctor for sickness and such, but for legal matters. And you know what? It's in a highrise, on the sixteenth floor. We have t'go up there in an elevator. I hope I don't get dizzy."

"Haven't you ever been in an elevator?"

Emmi shakes her head. "The doctor gets thirty marks a day for the apartment, for ten weeks," she says. "For one room with a kitchen."

"That's how it is in Berlin," says Lucie, shrugging. "It costs more. Ya, the smart and fancy folks. Many are called but few are chosen."

"But where does he stay the whole summer?" asks Emmi. "Does he have that much time to go on vacation?"

"Why not? Or who knows where all they might send him. He's in good with the authorities, otherwise he wouldn't be a doctor."

II

The day before yesterday Lucie saw a white sweater in a show window on Karl Marx Avenue. "Something like the one the Brummers' daughter Lore got from the West," she says.

The shop is closed, and Lucie hasn't been able to find the same one anywhere else. She's starting to panic.

"Over there, Emmi, doesn't that look like a sweater shop?" She grabs Emmi by the arm, pulls her across the street against a red light.

Emmi grumbles, her feet are hurting.

The sweater is actually there. Lucie is elated, then severely shaken. It doesn't fit.

With an imploring look, she asks the clerk: "Don't you really have a size larger?"

"No, I'm sorry."

To console herself, Lucie tries on other sweaters, debating whether or not she should buy each one.

Emmi, who has taken her shoes off, is sitting on a bench stretching out her toes.

"You are holding up all the other customers," says the clerk. "They want to use the fitting room too."

Lucie has a sleeveless blue sweater and a knitted dress set aside until closing time.

Outside she says to Emmi, who has rested feet and is in good spirits again: "They look good on me, don't you think? But I've already got so much stuff there isn't any more room in the closets. And maybe we'll find the white sweater in my size somewhere. Then Lore won't be strutting around so with hers anymore."

She takes Emmi in tow.

After standing in line for an hour and a half, they finally ride the elevator up to the restaurant in the Television Tower[2] and order several ice cream sundaes.

Emmi feels like staying put. "To look around a little bit," she says.

But Lucie urges, "The shops will be closing in two hours, and we still want to go to Köpenick."[3]

In Köpenick, a minute before closing time, she holds up the coveted treasure happily.

During supper Lucie unwraps the sweater and looks it over. She says, "It's a beauty, isn't it. I'll really turn some heads."

"Hm," says Emmi, "but I think you could've gotten it at home

2. A major landmark in the center of East Berlin, the Television Tower is 365 meters high.

3. A borough on the southeast edge of East Berlin, known for its wooded areas and waterways.

too. They had the same thing in the department store in Saal-feld."[4]

"What? Why didn't you say that in the beginning?"

"Maybe they'll be sold out when we get back, and then you'd have scolded me."

Emmi has eaten her fill and switches on the television. As she turns around to face Lucie, she sees the tears in her eyes. "What's the matter with you?"

"Oh, shut up," Lucie whimpers. "You always have to spoil my fun. This is the last trip I'm taking with you."

"I didn't mean to," says Emmi.

Lucie's tears flow. "It's not only because of the sweater," she gasps out between sobs. "Finally we're in Berlin, want t'see something, and what are we doing? Sitting in front of the tube."

"Let's try going to a bar once more."

"No, I've had enough. I won't put up with that again."

On the previous nights the two had dressed themselves up to celebrate. But there were long waiting lines in front of the bars.

"Well, we'll start out early tomorrow night," they had told each other. They had even been to the hairdresser, and at five-thirty, both in long dresses, they had set out for the restaurant bar called "Banquet of the Sea." The coat-check lady had recommended it to them at noon.

Lucie looked forward to the dancing most, Emmi to a chance to order trout.

They had stood at the entrance and waited to be shown to one of the many free tables. One hour later they were still waiting.

"But there are tables free," Lucie had said to the waiter for the third time.

"They are reserved, ladies."

When another hour had gone by, Lucie lost her patience.

Emmi whispered, "It's no use, Lucie. If they're reserved, they're reserved. Come, we'll go back and watch TV."

4. A city just to the northwest of the Thuringian Forest, in the *Bezirk* (or county) Gera.

Lucie stood with her arms akimbo, looking for the waiter. He was nowhere to be seen.

Emmi had tugged at the back of her blouse. "Come, Lucie, it's no use . . ."

"But tonight there's such a good program on," Emmi consoles her anew. "And at home I'm too tired to watch television in the evenings. I fall asleep during the most exciting mystery shows, while here . . ."

"Because you still romp around at work every day," Lucie mumbles. "But me . . . I'm bored the whole day, sit there like I'm glued to my chair and wait for one of the evening shows like the *Blaue Bock*[5] to come on. And now we're sitting in front of the tube here too." She starts to cry again.

"You don't want to go to the opera with me," Emmi says sadly. Then she has an idea. "We've got our crocheting along."

"What am I suppose t'crochet?" Lucie asks. "I already have everything, and there's no one I could give a present to."

"Crochet yourself a seat cover for your toilet, so it doesn't get so cold under your behind during the winter. Your toilet seat is like a piece of ice."

"You think so?"

They fetch their crocheting materials. They had brought them along in case it rained the whole time. While crocheting seat covers they watch TV.

III

The next morning Emmi says she'd like to go on a boatride.

"In the afternoon," Lucie says. "This morning I thought we'd look around in some more shops."

They trot across the steaming asphalt.

"Look at that beautiful glasswork," Emmi calls out, pointing at a show window.

"Oh, good, let's go inside!"

They look for an entrance. As Emmi opens the door she says, "It's an exhibition."

5. A musical variety show originating in West Germany.

[99]

"An exhibition? There's nothing to buy? Then we don't need to go in. What's the time? Isn't it soon time to eat?"

"Only quarter to eleven, Lucie. I'm not hungry yet."

They sit down on a bench, stretch their legs out, and yawn, then size up the people strolling by.

"Look what she has on," Lucie observes. "God almighty. And that one. She's not even wearing a brassiere. The morals they have here."

Eleven-thirty. They are sitting in the rathskeller, waiting for menus. Lucie orders wild duck with dumplings, Emmi beefsteak with fried potatoes and vegetables.

"And this afternoon you're going to buy that ring on Unter den Linden,[6] the one with the green stone. You really liked that one."

Emmi shakes her head. "It's too expensive. Elke is starting school, I want to get something nice for her."

"And the one with coral? That costs only 300."

"Such a huge thing. It's not right for my hand."

Before they set out for Treptow[7] and the steamer cruise in the afternoon, Lucie wants to go back to the apartment again. "I want to put something different on. I have to wear everything I brought along at least once."

While changing, she warbles: "This is the kind of life I like, beautiful clothes, jewelry, and good food. Whoever's got that can be happy. Don't I look classy? She steps in front of Emmi, who's been sitting on the john for the last quarter of an hour, and models.

Emmi smiles, showing her honest approval.

They set out.

They miss the first steamer because Lucie discovers an arts and crafts shop at the subway exit. As a souvenir of the trip she buys a wood carving with the motto *While The World Outside May*

6. The main thoroughfare of East Berlin, historically famous for its linden trees.

7. A borough of East Berlin bordering on the river Spree.

Run Its Race, My Home Shall Be My Resting Place. The two lines
are entwined with violets.

There is another boat a quarter of an hour later. They storm on
board to get the best seats. Lucie opens her umbrella to shade
them from the sun. They sit next to each other, Emmi hunched
up in her sweaty blouse and crumpled blue skirt, Lucie decked
out like a queen in an expensive dress of flowery silk.

They have fallen into an argument.

"Oh, if only I could bring Bruno back," Lucie moans. "So I'd
have someone to cook for. I'm so alone."

"Yes," Emmi replies, "but you had Bruno for thirty years. I've
been alone since the war."

"What did you need a husband for?" Lucie shakes her head.
"You had your son, now you have a daughter-in-law and grand-
son that you can leave something to. What have you missed?"

Her friend smiles, then says: "Well, just what a husband and
wife have together."

"Oh, nonsense," Lucie says and gives Emmi a poke in the side.
"You haven't missed a thing. I'd have been happy if I'd had my
peace and quiet at night. At least you had that."

Emmi blushes, looks down at the toes of her shoes and says,
"No, Lucie, I had my husband for a while too. I know how it is."

"Oh, come now, you didn't miss a thing." With her hand full of
heavy rings Lucie slaps her friend on the arm.

Emmi is silent and looks at the private cottages on both sides
of the narrow canal they are passing through. The water laps
against the colorful boats tied up to the boat docks.

As Lucie starts to cry, Emmi consoles her. "You'll see, you'll
find another husband. No one's going to take your Mr. Right
away from you."

"No, you don't think so?" Lucie whispers. She puts one arm
around Emmi's shoulder and with her other hand wipes away her
own tears. "How nice we made this trip together. You know
what? Shouldn't we go to the opera tonight? You listen to the
singing and I'll have a look at people's clothes."

Emmi is happy. Then she points at the surrounding view and says, "The lakes here are even prettier than I'd imagined. It makes me feel good, too, to give my feet a rest. Doesn't mean anything to you, but at work I always stand on one foot. With the other one I operate the crank lever. So my feet just aren't the same anymore."

"You poor thing," Lucie sighs.

On the way back they inquire at the Berlin Information Office about the evening's program at the opera.

"Sorry," says the young woman behind the ticket window, "it's summer time. The theaters are closed."

Emmi has looked forward too much to the evening. Her face grows pale. Now it's Lucie's turn to console. "Maybe there'll be an opera on television tonight. They show lots of them. And if not, we'll crochet and just make ourselves at home."

IV

The following day is Sunday, the day of departure.

They pack their suitcases early in the morning. Lucie looks hers over and moans. "What if it bursts open?"

"Don't worry," Emmi says soothingly, "it'll be all right."

They want to attend the worship service in the little church nearby, where yesterday they had studied the month's program posted on the front door.

The minister is very young. His mustache and his unkempt, shoulder-length hair are appalling to Lucie, but she has to admit she likes his sermon. About the meaning of a life that not only . . . you can never allow yourself to become too comfortable . . .

Then they join in the singing with gusto, proud that they know the song text by heart. Lucie sobs while she sings: "Oh, how fleeting, oh, how vain is earthly joy / Like a ball / One time here it stops, one time there / So with earthly joy . . ."

"We sang that at Bruno's funeral too, remember?"

Emmi nods.

Their train is scheduled to depart in the afternoon. Although the station is only ten minutes away, Lucie insists they start out two hours early. "In case my suitcase bursts open on the way, we can still pack everything in sacks," she says.

As they are standing in front of the elevator with their luggage, a young woman approaches.

"You live next door, don't you?" asks Lucie. "Is Dr. Helm usually gone so much? We haven't seen him once."

"Oh no," the woman says, "he doesn't live here. He's got a house in Biesdorf.[8] This is his stopover place. He probably doesn't need it during the summer."

After the woman has left the elevator, Lucie says: "And I thought he sublet his apartment so in Berlin we'd have a chance . . ."

Emmi scratches her arm thoughtfully. "But the apartment, it had a beautiful bathroom, you have to admit that."

"Yes," says Lucie, "when I sat in there in the mornings, it was the most beautiful thing in all of Berlin. You know what? We'll come back here in the fall. In a hotel. I'll pay your share."

8. A suburban area of East Berlin in the borough of Lichtenberg. Dr. Helm's two residences point up the existence of a privileged class in the GDR.

Street Sweepers

·

"Go easy, it's a long night."

After two hours these are the first words I hear from the older man who shares my shift assignment.

"In this cold not many people sit on the benches. Isn't much trash today."

Broom in hand, I lean against the base of the Television Tower and observe my partner as he lifts my little pile of cigarette butts, ice cream sticks, and dried dog turds with a light push of his shovel and dumps it out over the handcart.

He doesn't look left or right, stares only at the ground. Although he's the only one of the street sweepers not wearing the orange vest—instead he's got on a turtleneck sweater and half-way decent cotton trousers—his walk, his look, and the evenness of his movements seem to chain him to the handcart and broom.

During the shift assignments someone muttered to me: "He's an old grouch, you'll get bored."

I had noticed how he grimaced, disappointed, when the boss read out: "Kramer. Eckart. Television Tower," instead of the usual: "Kramer. The pedestrian tunnels."

I go back to work. The looks I get from all directions don't interest me anymore.

Evening comes on.

The shadows of the pedestrians grow longer. Among them are

[104]

many Arabs from West Berlin heading for the cafés and disco-theques.[1]

Their footsteps sound like courting signals.

"Over there they're treated like shit," says my partner, "and here they think they're kings."

As I reach for my shovel atop the handcart, he beats me to it again, and with the same movement as before makes my garbage pile disappear in the container.

One of the Arabs stops, looks at me. Then he says, "You a pretty young lady, why you do this?"

"To earn some money," I say, "to add to my scholarship."

"How much you get?"

"For twelve hours on the weekend, 61 marks."

"West?"

"Of course not."

His eyes open wide. "61 GDR marks? Is little. But you, pretty young lady. Others old as you earn money easier." From his pocket he fishes out notepaper and ballpoint pen. "Where you live? I give you for one hour 50 marks . . . West."[2]

I shake my head and knock against his shiny dress shoes with the broom. Between them lies a flattened bottle cap.

"You don't interest me," I say.

He jumps back, then circles around me, looking me over suspiciously from head to foot.

"She's not a humpback," my partner growls at him.

It surprises me. It's his third comment of the evening.

He sweeps, jerkily now, his face showing embarrassment.

1. Foreign workers in West Berlin, many of them single males from Turkey and Arabic countries, often traveled to East Berlin in search of female companionship and recreation. Their access to Western goods and currency made them more popular than otherwise might have been the case. On occasion the Germans may refer to all such foreign workers as "Arabs."

2. On the black market one could easily get 6 GDR marks for 1 West German mark. In other words, the Arab's offer to the narrator is more than fifty times her hourly rate as a street sweeper.

The Arab leaves.

My partner throws his broom and shovel into the handcart and for the first time looks me in the face. "It's no use now. When the disco lets out everything'll be dirty again. Wanna come along and have a cup a' coffee?"

He pushes the handcart into the alcove at the base of the tower.

We stop at a café on the Square.[3]

"And if an inspector comes?" I ask.

"Ulli's boss today. He never comes before midnight."

Before we go in he studies the customers uneasily, then he says, "It's okay here."

We sit down at one of the out-of-the-way tables.

The waitress comes. He orders two large coffees. "And some ice cream?"

I nod.

"What kind?" the waitress asks, handing me the menu.

My partner offers me a cigarette.

"I've got my own," I say and put the pack on the table. It seems to offend him.

I take one of his cigarettes. We smoke.

"It's very nice here," I say.

He remains quiet, looks at his cigarette.

The coffee comes. He drinks greedily.

The dish of ice cream has a high mound of whipped cream with a chocolate on the top.

"It really looks good," I say.

"Enjoy it," my partner says almost in a whisper. He doesn't look up from his cigarette.

"You aren't really mute, like the others say." I smile at him as he looks up briefly.

When he orders two more coffees, I tell him how hard it was for me to get used to Berlin when I started at the university. He begins to listen.

3. Alexander-Platz, at the center of East Berlin.

After a while he says, "I've got a daughter your age. And two more younger ones. They cling to their mother, . . . hardly see 'em. But Roswitha comes by pretty often. She's a secretary for Robotron."[4]

"Are you divorced?"

"For six years. I like t'take a nip once in a while. It got to the wife. I can understand. A shame. The wife wasn't bad. It's mainly bars and alcohol do me in." Again he stares for a long time at his cigarette.

"How so?" I want to keep the conversation going.

"I was a soccer player. A good one, too. Had it set up so I could study physical education. Wanted to be a coach. But just before the examination, . . . well, it's bad when you like the booze too much." With a feeble motion he shoos a fly off the edge of his cup.

"And then what did you do?"

He answers with a thankful look, as if he couldn't talk without being asked.

"Truck driver," he says, "twenty years for a coal outfit. But in March I got mine. Too much alcohol in the blood. Already the third time. There went my driver's license. Two years before I'll get it back again."

"Oh well, until then you can earn something at this job. Here the pay's better and you can show up whenever you want to."

"This is no job," he replies. "Besides, in the mornings you're too worn out. The whole day's wasted when you get so worn out. Yesterday morning I fell asleep in the train headed for Schöne-weide, that's where I live, and I rode back and forth between Friedrich Street and Schönefeld until noon."[5]

"Then go to work on the day shift."

4. VEB Kombinat Robotron, a state-owned computer manufacturer with headquarters in Dresden, GDR.

5. Schöneweide is a suburban area of East Berlin bordering on the boroughs of Treptow and Köpenick. Friedrich Street and Schöenfeld are the first and last stations on the commuter train line that runs from downtown East Berlin to Schöneweide.

He shakes his head. "If somebody I know sees me. . . . That's why I'm sweepin' here, not in Schöneweide."

"And another job?"

"I'm on the lookout. Found somethin' too. In a *Kulturhaus*,[6] furnace man and general caretaker. But . . ." He shrugs, forgets my presence again.

His face is full of black stubbles. His eyes dull and dispirited.

"If you like taking a nip so much, why are you having coffee now? The others surely drink during working hours."

"You won't squeal?" He smiles for the first time and waves to the waitress. "A beer for you, too?" he asks.

"I don't like beer."

"Schnapps?"

I nod.

He orders two double shots and a large draft beer. He looks at me as if I should ask him about something else.

"At Pentecost,[7] during the festival, street cleaners all got large bonuses. Everyone was there but you."

"I was locked up then," he says without raising his voice.

"Why was that?"

"On the night before Pentecost I went out for a nip. Back there at the big table me and a couple a' buddies were playin' skat.[8] After twelve it struck me: the cleanin' crew's sittin' under the Television Tower. They were really out there too, gabbin' and puffin' away. I had the cards along. We played a hand of skat, then another one. Then a policeman come along, hand on his belt. Two minutes later he comes by again. The fat guy, the one who pushes the road brush across the Square, smarts off to him. He gets it back. Right away they're at each other. I step between 'em. 'Don't be an idiot,' I say to Fatty. Just then another policeman

6. A *Kulturhaus* is a state-sponsored educational and recreational center. See note 2 of "The Tall Girl."

7. *Pfingsten*, a traditional German holiday.

8. A popular German card game with three players and thirty-two playing cards.

comes. Somebody yells, 'the pigs!' Then all hell broke loose. After I'd sobered up I was supposed t'admit I was the guilty one. 'It wasn't me!' I say. 'Oh yes it was!' they said. 'Your work crew testified to it.'"

"Was it bad being locked up?" I ask.

"Only six weeks. I volunteered for work. My cellmates said, 'You're crazy. Get a good rest in here.' But when you're doin' somethin' the time goes faster, and besides . . . if I don't work I don't feel human. The first week I washed vegetables. Then a cook got sick. I had to take over pots and pans, not only for the jailbirds but those for the bigshots too. That's how I learned to cook. Even carp I can do . . ."

We're quiet for a long time.

"I've got a small place," he continues, "in a new building. An efficiency with kitchen and bathroom. Looks out on a park. You can really feel at home there. And a few years ago I found another lady friend. But when she didn't hear nothin' from me for six weeks, she thought: the guy took off. And what's she do? Turns my place into a whorehouse. Now I have another friend. She's different. And she likes to take a nip too. That's good. Then you don't get carried away. And at skat she can beat any man. . . . Only she doesn't know . . . that I've done time and that I'm pushin' a broom. What woman wants such a . . . I'm payin'!"

"Put it away," he says bruskly as I take out my wallet.

Then we're back at our handcart.

I sweep the steps around the Neptune Fountain. The wind sprays the water over the fountain's edge. Cigarette butts paddle around in puddles. I move them to shore. My broom paints big curlicues. I see no one.

"Not a soul on the Square either," say the others already trudging toward the gathering place.

In the lounge an old street sweeper shoos me out of my chair. "It's mine, the part-timers sit in back."

I change places, rest a bit, then go to wash up. Coming back I notice on the table in front of me a large coffee and a plate with bockwurst and bread.

The boy at the table opposite looks up from his book and says in a strong Saxon[9] accent: "From the guy over there, the one you're on duty with."

I nod my thanks across to him and carry over two of the peaches that I stood in line for in the morning.[10]

He takes them.

He sits by himself at the table. Whoever happens to come near him hesitates, then moves a few tables farther on.

The murmur of voices makes me sleepy.

Chairs scrape.

"Back to work," says the boy.

When he sees me sticking my belongings into my bag, he adds, "Why always pack your stuff away? Nobody steals here."

At work my partner admonishes me again: "Easy, six o'clock is still a long ways off."

About ten-thirty I feel the first blister on my right hand.

I look more often at the city hall clock. The big hand seems to be stuck.

A man passes with a tiny dog that needs to pee once more, then a policeman goes past. Shortly before midnight a soldier sprints by, looking as though he's running for his life.

We take a smoke break.

"Don't the roses look good with the lights shinin' up like that?" my partner observes coolly. "You're goin' too fast. You'll wear yourself out, and besides there's not enough trash."

"I'm cold. Have to keep moving."

He looks over at me. "You don't have enough clothes on."

We gaze up at the sky. It's cloudless. The stars sparkle like splintered glass.

9. *Sächsisch*, a dialect spoken in Saxony, southeastern GDR. See note 21 of "Feldberg and Back." The boy's accent reveals that he, like the narrator, is an outsider.

10. A reference to the scarcity of fresh fruit in East German stores.

In the dance café under the Television Tower the lights go out. The last couples are leaving.

"The disco's out. Start in by the tower, you've got protection from the wind there."

From one o'clock on I feel total exhaustion. I'm cold and sweep like a robot.

I picture myself always having to work this way, and suddenly I understand how *taking a nip* can mean pure bliss. The big hand jumps to 1:30.

The second break. I sleep through it with my eyes open. A shrill voice awakens me: "What are the canteen floozies for if they can't even warm up a bockwurst?"

On the way to the handcart my partner offers me another cigarette.

"I can't," I say. "My God, how you guys smoke. One night shift and my chest will ache for three days."

As I turn the corner on the landing outside the Television Tower, a gust of wind nearly knocks me down.

Then I scan the horizon for the first ray of sun. When you wake up in the afternoon, I tell myself consolingly, all of it will only have been a dream.

My partner sweeps the same steps for the third time. Our trash pile wouldn't outweigh a feather.

"Let's see how you're doin'," he says as we're standing opposite each other under a street light. "You're all blue! Go in the train station and warm up. The inspection's over."

"And you?"

He shakes his head, continues sweeping.

Once inside the station, I understand why.

The street sweepers are squatting or leaning against the ticket counters. In the fluorescent light, against the glaring orange of their vests, their faces look powdery white. I'm among ghosts.

At the end of the row the boy who sat across from me during the break squats on the floor, a book on his knees.

Reading, he sees and hears nothing else.

I feel spineless as a jellyfish.

They say hello, willingly make room for me. I warm myself in their company. Listen to their chatter. I'm starting to feel better.

A very heavy, thick-set man with a face like a clump of dirt is speaking. The one who pushes the road brush over the Square every night. The others look at him submissively. He's standing next to me.

"Do you have the longest time in here?" I ask.

"Almost, after that guy there." He points at a thin young man with drooping lower lip. I'd guess him to be in his late twenties. "He's been street cleanin' fourteen years now, and me just eleven. Worked on a pig farm, the outskirts of Berlin. New development there now. I didn't wanna go no farther out. So haul yourself to town, I says, see what's goin' on."

Our conversation ebbs. Fatty offers me a cigarette. I don't dare refuse.

I think of my partner who's outside cleaning the flagstones.

Fatty guesses where my mind is. "It got boring with that grouch, huh?" He exhales contentedly.

I feel myself getting angry. "A grouch? Why call him that?"

"What're you gettin' at?"

"Who was it that called the policeman a pig the night before Pentecost and then shoved the blame on him? Got him thrown in the slammer because of it." I'm shocked at my own voice.

"He's been singin'!" says an old guy and laughs. "Otherwise he can't get his yap open, and to this young one . . ."

A tall guy with a big round belly that looks like a melon stuffed under his vest paces restlessly back and forth. His pants legs are way too short, exposing his thin calves and his large flipperlike shoes.

He turns to the old one. "Haven't ya got a smoke?"

The old guy gives him a pacifying wink as he lights his cigarette.

"Why's that make 'im such a grouch all of a sudden?" the old guy asks me. "Like his wife croaked on 'im or somethin'. Six weeks . . . ain't even a baptism for a street cleaner."

The boy looks up from his book. "You sent him to jail?"

"What's six weeks?" The old guy laughs.

A girl, a trainee for the State Railroad who is part-timing here, shouts, "You bastards!"

At Pentecost she seemed stronger to me, more ruddy-cheeked. Now she looks like an old woman. Three weeks ago she lost her wallet in the tram, 600 marks in it, and since then she's been working almost every night shift.

She straightens up in order to say more, then spits in front of the tall guy.

The boy with the drooping lip grins.

"Shut your trap," says the old one. "You're still too green for that stuff." He scratches his neck, then says regretfully: "Wasn't nothin' else to do that day. The guy that let the name slip out has a record. Four convictions. He wouldn't'a got off with six weeks."

"What a reason!" the boy with the book says in disgust.

The old guy answers with a yawn.

A gaunt woman says hoarsely, "Franz, we shoulda . . . maybe . . . shoulda we said we'z sorry?"

Fatty says nothing.

"Well, doncha think, Franz, . . ." the woman repeats, "we shoulda at least told 'im? . . ."

Fatty shoves a fresh cigarette in his mouth.

Tension hangs in the air.

Fatty puffs away leisurely. The crisis starts to ease. They are smoking again, chatting, looking at their watches.

Morning creeps above the rooftops. Pedestrians with tired faces, even more tired than ours, trudge by to the early shift. No one pays attention to us.

The boy with the drooping lip points out at the flower beds. "The pigeons, look at 'em, they're eatin' the flowers. We shoulda trained 'em to eat butts."

[113]

"Ha, then we'd have it easy," somebody bawls out. The others snicker.

"I'm going to see how my partner's doing." I leave.

"Drag 'im in here," Fatty calls after me good-naturedly. "Otherwise he'll sweep a hole in the Square. Tell 'im we *invite* him to come."

I find my partner behind the Neptune Fountain. "Everything's clean here. Come along inside."

He goes on as if he hasn't heard anything.

"Come on!" I walk at his side. "Come with me. The others are inviting you to. You can't always stay by yourself . . ."

I tell him quickly about the conversation inside.

His face remains expressionless.

"What are you studyin'?" he asks.

"Philosophy . . . come on!"

Nodding, he says, "And here you're studyin' for real."

He glances up briefly, I smile at him. He trods on. I follow him. "You'll freeze to death out here. I'll finish it myself," he says harshly.

I repeat the invitation to come along until the monotony of his movements silences me.

Just in front of the train station I turn around to look once more.

Swinging the broom, he's growing smaller and smaller.

In Saubersdorf, beyond Glauchau

.

Riding the night train from Gdansk to Berlin.[1] Though I am tired, I haven't been able to fall asleep. Ever since our departure two hours ago, the two married couples in the compartment have been poking around in their luggage. Now they have yet another idea, to stuff half of their suitcases under the seat. They ask me to stand up. For the umpteenth time I hear, "Customs!"

I pick up my bag and leave. Maybe I can find a calmer place in another compartment.

I have good luck in the very next one. In the dim light I can make out a woman sleeping. She's small, a bit plump, in her forties. On her lap the head of a young girl with black, curly hair who lies stretched out dreaming in her sleep.

A dark landscape fills the compartment as it goes flying past. Now and then a lighted window.

I lie down on the unoccupied seats across from the woman and close my eyes.

A few hours later I'm awakened by the sound of screeching brakes. Border. Customs.

An official turns on the light.

Aroused, the woman searches her dress pocket warily for her passport, trying not to awaken the child.

I sit up, also take out my passport. My glance passes over the

1. Before the emergence of the Solidarity movement in Poland in the 1980s, it was relatively easy for GDR citizens to travel to Poland and vice versa.

woman. She is pale, has thin, dull hair, a bland face. I yawn and am about to close my eyes again when the woman looks at me.

Her look . . . is peculiar. I become attentive. It is so proud, so confident, that her whole face changes. The features become clear, decisive.

The door opens. A GDR border policeman enters, a tall, gangly young man with a beard of peach fuzz.

The woman hands him her passport. He gestures for her to wake the child. She shakes her gently. The girl rubs her eyes, stares groggily into the compartment.

The glances of the uniformed young man shift skeptically back and forth between mother and child. The girl is a mulatto, tall for her age, broad-shouldered, with an alert, dark-skinned face. He pages through her passport again, asks for the second time: "*Your* child?" Finally he wants to hear from the girl herself what her name is.

"Ayane Morgner," she says and looks at him angrily.

The Polish border policeman, a portly man with a curly red mustache doesn't make a big issue of the passports. He winks at the girl in a friendly way. She smiles back. Then she says, "Look!" She opens her right fist and shows him a small plastic cat. He pretends to be surprised, winks at her once more before he leaves.

"There's another customs check," says the woman, "then you can sleep some more."

Full of energy, the girl climbs down from the seat, shoves the curtain away from the window, flattens her nose against the glass.

Outside the day dawns. Trees and villages are sketched fleetingly at the window.

"I'm hungry, Mommy," the girl says with the same Saxon[2] accent as the woman.

"Yes, me too. Sit over here." The woman unpacks sandwiches

2. See note 21 of "Feldberg and Back"; the dialect is from the southeastern part of the GDR.

and pastries from a bag, stacks them up on a clean handkerchief between herself and the child.

I take out my lunch sack. My girlfriend, I notice, has even stuck a marmalade glass full of freshly washed strawberries in my briefcase.

The child stops eating her cake, stares at the glass.

"Have some," I say encouragingly and reach the glass across.

She responds without hesitating, offers one of the berries to the woman.

"You eat it," says the woman in a kind voice.

The woman strokes the child tenderly over her stiff, curly hair as she devours the strawberries, smacking her lips with pleasure.

Beaming, she says, "Thank you" after she has finished. Comes over, opens her fist and also lets me see the plastic cat. Then she reflects on something, says a few words, and in a whirl of arms and legs suddenly she's sitting up on the luggage shelf and looking down at me happily. Her face, marred by a rough complexion, is not pretty. But her eyes are unusually alert and imaginative. All of a sudden she seems beautiful to me. I nod appreciatively.

The woman doesn't know if she should laugh or scold. "But Ayane," she calls out, "come down!"

The girl climbs down leisurely, resumes her place. She snuggles her head against the woman's shoulder and hums contentedly. The woman puts her arm around her.

She is aware that I'm watching. She looks at me, as if searching for ulterior motives. Then she clears her throat and gives me another one of those confident looks that I find puzzling.

Curious, the girl sticks her head out into the corridor. "I'm going to walk up and down a little, Mommy," she says.

"But not too far." The woman leans back in her corner.

I smile at her. She looks away. After a while she says, "She's a happy child, don't you think?"

When I agree, she breathes a sigh of relief.

"Is she your child?" I ask.

She nods emphatically, then she says: "I adopted Ayane. No one wanted her. But a child is a child, I thought, and I've brought her up."

She smiles. "In Saubersdorf, beyond Glauchau."[3]

3. A village near the city of Glauchau, located in the extreme southern part of the GDR.

Uncle Benno

.

There was to be a wedding at home in the Erz highlands.[1]
I traveled the 300 kilometers from a metropolis to the village.
The bridal couple were two of my cousins and this made the
family happy: the dowry and later the inheritance would remain
in the hands of relatives.

The inn "Rehbock" was rented for the reception.

After the ceremony in the church, the bridegroom and the
bride sawed through a fir trunk, sweating amid the hearty laughter of onlookers in front of the inn.[2] Then we entered the hall.
Garlands were stretched from lamp to lamp, large bouquets of
asters decorated the window benches. On the tables, carnations
were scattered among the place settings, namecards, menus, and
the bottles of Grauer-Mönch wine.

We were forty guests. The day before, on the eve of the
wedding, the entire village had tapped beer in the garden behind
my uncle's house and smashed all the bottles and glasses of the
world against the garden wall.[3] This wedding was to cost 5,000
marks so that people would have cause to talk about it for a long
time.

After all the guests had finally found their places and were

1. *Erzgebirge*, a mountain range on the border between the GDR and
Czechoslovakia.

2. An old German marriage custom.

3. *Polterabend*, a party held traditionally on the evening before a wedding
when dishes are smashed.

studying the menus, the first of the five courses was brought in. My grandfather examined the flaky pastry from all sides, then consulted the menu. "Aha, Rago-ut," he said with an air of importance. He pronounced it the way it's spelled.

Uncle Benno, who sat opposite me at the table, grinned. "It's called ragout, Otto," he said. "It's a French word." He sampled the fare. "Hm. Made with beef."

The women wore floor-length lace dresses in purple, salmon pink, and turquoise. The men had on dark suits, white shirts, and ties in loud colors. After eating, they opened the top buttons of their shirts and trousers.

Uncle Benno, who enjoyed entertaining the others, pointed at the bridal couple. "Look at that, the way they smooch. They'll never have to work, they won't have time."

"You don't hafta work either, Willy," my aunt said to her husband. "Tell about how often . . ."

"Ya, always when there's money, then I'm popular."

Others snicker.

"Well, that *is* something special whenever there's money," says my aunt sulkily.

Uncle Benno, who seemed pleased that I sat across from him, was amused and winked at me.

It became quiet.

"Here comes the music," somebody called out.

Bodo, the singer and accordian player who performed at every celebration in the village, stepped through the doorway of the hall.

He set his accordian on a chair and mumbled a greeting to the guests, lowering his glance as if he were trying out an invisible microphone. Instead of congratulations, he expressed his sympathy to the bridal couple.

He took up the instrument, nonchalantly pulled it open and then tilted his head to one side.

Tall and raw-boned, Bodo had a lax bearing. The most noticeable things about him were his long neck with the large Adam's apple and his small head, unruly hair, and curiously glowing eyes. He sang folksongs, partly in high German, partly in dialect. The better ones, the sad old melodies, he parodied in a strange way, as if he were refusing to offer them to the satiated wedding party. He sang tenor, his voice going higher and higher before he finally yodeled, everything there was to yodel, and always he shifted abruptly into the refrain: "So let's go a-rowing, / So let's go a-sailing, / So let's go a-riding our little boat / On the high sea . . ."

Uncle Benno stiffened. Then he fidgeted about on the edge of his chair and looked between his legs at the floor. Something seemed to unsettle him. He was sweating and wiped his bald head with a handkerchief. He stared at the place behind me where the singing came from. His mouth quivered.

The waiter brought over a tray with cognac purchased in one of the shops for export goods,[4] 80 marks a bottle. Uncle Benno took a glass and emptied it in one gulp. He screwed up his mouth, looking as if he'd swallowed cod-liver oil.

He had stomach problems and normally never drank alcohol.

"What's wrong, Uncle Benno, don't you feel well?" I asked.

He didn't hear me. He stared at Bodo.

I thought maybe he was hearing him for the first time. It was possible. Many years ago, after the death of his wife, he had moved into his sister's neighborhood with his books and his music. He never went out, and had shown up today only at the special request of the bridal couple. He was a godfather to both.

Once again he downed a cognac, and judging from the look on his face it must have tasted worse than the first.

I tried it. The cognac was exquisite.

Bodo was playing "So let's go a-rowing / So let's go a-sailing . . ." again. Everyone linked arms and sang along with the music. Uncle Benno, music teacher and director of the large school chorus until his retirement, normally took advantage of

4. *Feinkostgeschäft.*

every opportunity to sing but now was silent. My two aunts, sitting on each side of him, had grabbed his arms and his body swayed back and forth between them.

After the swinging stopped, he had his arms free and reached for a new glass.

The father of the groom gave a formal speech and the dancing began. Bodo played waltzes, transforming the well-fed guests into jubilant, bounding merrymakers. Even the older ones joined in.

After the first three sets, Bodo let the dancers catch their breath. He sang one of those half-folksongs that I nevertheless like, the one about the rowan tree.[5] Here again he adorned the melody with ironic flourishes that made the guests laugh.

My father led me to the dance floor. I was surprised that Bodo's voice could still be heard over the scraping of forty pairs of shoes. Recently, my father said, there was someone in the village from the Leipzig Opera. He wanted to take Bodo under his wing and see that he got proper training. Bodo turned him down, said he was almost forty and besides in music he'd gotten a "D."

I danced next with the groom. When it became too warm, I asked him to accompany me to the bar. The bride's sister, who was expecting, was playing barmaid. Uncle Benno was her sole customer. He was drinking cognac again, making a face as if he'd been ordered to drink from the poisoned cup.

Soon the others came over to join us and began telling jokes. "Did you know that nowadays the names of aborted children are being entered in the parents' passports? No, why's that? They go under the heading 'Distant Relatives'. . . . A snail and a billy goat wanted to get into heaven, but there was only room for one. So God sets up a race and says the winner goes to heaven. They both take off, and as the billy goat, sweatin' and complainin', arrives at the finish line, the snail's already there. Now do you believe me, when I say you get farther with crawlin' than with complain-

5. "*Mei Vuchelbeerbaam*" (*Mein Vogelbeerbaum*).

in'? . . . Miss Blackbird wants to get married, Mr. Fox think's he's the chosen one. 'No,' she says, 'it's the little Sandman. He comes every night . . ."[6]

The laughter grew louder after every punch line.

I looked at Uncle Benno. He didn't laugh. His blue eyes were dull and he looked uneasily in the direction the music was coming from. Drops of sweat stood out on his bald head.

The joke machine ran on. An elderly lady giggled. "Stop, or I'll wet my pants!"

Then the material gave out.

Someone remembered Benno. "Come on, Benno. You always know the best ones!"

Uncle Benno started up, reflected.

Then he said, "What does a person from the GDR do if he sees a snake in the desert?"

"But Benno, we just heard that one. He gets into line, of course. Don't you know any others?"

Benno shook his head. Then he turned again toward the bar. "Could I have another one?"

Everybody laughed as if he'd told a good joke.

"At seventy ol' Benno's startin' to nip."

Bodo went on another break. The jokes switched to the moderately erotic.

Uncle Benno, who was normally fond of such jokes, shuffled away from the group.

Bodo had taken a seat at one of the empty tables. He was having coffee and a piece of cake. Uncle Benno stopped in front of him.

Bodo glanced up, continued eating. Then he shoved the rest of the cake into his mouth, rose to his feet and walked past Uncle Benno and out of the hall.

Uncle Benno lowered his head, held on to the table.

6. A reference to the nightly television program for children in the GDR, "*Unser Sandmännchen*" (Our Little Sandman).

Then he turned and followed after Bodo.

He didn't get as far as the door.

In the meantime the conversation at the bar had turned to spare parts. Somebody said, "I need a new bathtub. Schulz, who's got a couple, says, 'Get me twenty heating pipes and one of the tubs is yours.' But where am I gonna find heating pipes? I need some myself. I'll hafta get somebody t'write a letter to city hall for me. Benno can do it, he knows how."

He followed Uncle Benno, caught him by the arm. "Don't you run away! You've been at the bottle since this morning . . ."

He pulled Uncle Benno along.

Soon we were sitting at our places again. A procession of gaily dressed women entered through the doorway of the hall. Up front were two very old ones in wide, colorfully embroidered skirts, ornamental white caps on their heads. One of them carried a basket full of live pigeons, the other held a collection of brightly colored ribbons on her outstretched arms.

They stopped in front of the bridal couple.

The one with the ribbons recited proverbs in a clear, solemn voice. For each proverb her companion released a pigeon.[7]

Then they switched roles.

The ribbons were wound around the necks of the bridal couple, drawing them closer together. The old woman who had recited earlier was sniveling. The other one, gasping for air, read out a line for each ribbon: "Fiery red is the flame of love / May it never be extinguished / For the ribbon of love holds you together / May happiness remain forever in your home . . ." She cleared her throat, repeated again and again: "The Lord God, may he preserve you . . ."

The groom had to prompt her: "The Lord God, may he be with you."

Then the women sat down and it was Bodo's turn again.

7. A traditional ceremony at wedding celebrations in the region of Vogtland in the GDR.

He left the accordian behind, walked to the center of the hall and sang, without accompaniment, Tamino's aria, "This Portrait Is Enchantingly Beautiful."[8] For the first time he sang without ironic embellishments.

"That's art," someone whispered. Others were eating again and would have preferred something comical. Uncle Benno listened with slightly opened mouth, then he groaned.

Applause.

"Let's hear another one!" called the young man who had just whispered. Benno stood up and hurried out of the hall as if he feared a beating. No one paid any attention.

I liked Uncle Benno because of his passion for music and his large bookcase. No one else among our relatives had so many books. And Uncle Benno loved children. After school he had often brought an entire horde home with him and beamed when they climbed in his apple trees or played cops and robbers. School was easy for me, textbooks I found boring. Many times I'd stood before Uncle Benno's bookcase and it obviously pleased him.

When I reached the age of twelve, he let me correct his pupils' essays and math problems. After I had everything right, he walked solemnly over to the bookcase, opened it and began setting up a tower of books on the table: fairy tales, paintings by Raphael and Titian, biographies of famous musicians. Alongside them he placed a shoebox labeled *Men's Sandals*. It contained chocolates.

Almost everyday after school I rode to the neighboring village to visit Uncle Benno. On the weekends I stayed over and helped him with garden work in the morning. Then he taught me how to play the piano.

I walked out of the hall and found Uncle Benno on a birch-log bench behind the inn.

He sat staring at the toes of his shoes. There were large bags under his eyes.

8. From Mozart's *Die Zauberflöte* (The Magic Flute).

"Can I be of help?" I asked.

He didn't stir, then shook his head.

I decided to go for a walk.

It was muggy, the air lay like a sponge over the countryside. I had trouble walking in my long dress.

Once again I stood in front of the bench.

"Was this the first time you heard Bodo sing?" I asked.

Uncle Benno said nothing. After a while he looked at me.

"I am an ass, Birgit," he said.

I laughed. "You are the friendliest man in the world. You just can't drink cognac."

"No," he said. "Twenty-five years ago I discovered Bodo's voice. The boy was shy. I gave him encouragement, sent him to the district music contest. He came back with better results than we'd hoped for, his name was in the paper. . . . The school superintendent called me in: Bodo, he reminded me, was the son of a church officer,[9] hadn't even been in the Pioneers . . ."[10]

"And what did I do? I said to the boy, 'No use to get big-headed, you're not as good as you think you are.'"

He was silent. Then he added, "And here I thought I'd forgotten about it."

9. A reflection of the cultural and ideological struggle waged between church and state in the GDR.

10. The Ernst Thälmann Pioneer Organization, a junior wing of Free German Youth (FDJ, see note 7 of "Old Woman"), for boys and girls in the GDR between six and fourteen years of age. Membership reached 1.8 million in 1975. Like the Free German Youth, the Pioneers combined political indoctrination with recreational activities.

Hitchhiking

·

It is early November, the air heavy and grayish-blue like fish spawn.

After standing along the entrance to the expressway for an hour, I run in place in order to keep my feet warm.

In this weather there's hardly any traffic, and furthermore I'm only visible from a distance of several meters. A blurred outline with backpack and umbrella.

A transport truck approaches. Going fifty kilometers an hour at most. Doesn't matter. I raise my hand.

I have to say that I don't often hitchhike. When I do, then I prefer trucks. The drivers who've been on the road a long time appreciate the chance to talk a bit. Keeps them from falling asleep at the wheel.

The truck with its heavy trailer stops a few meters in front of me. I close the umbrella, the door of the cab opens from inside. I call up where I want to go.

The driver, chubby, middle-aged, nods.

Grinning, he watches how I climb up on the high seat. Then, as he takes a closer look at me, he seems surprised. We start out.

I take off my wet parka, make myself comfortable.

The road surface is in miserable shape.

"Expressway? A washboard," sighs the driver. "Could get your insides all twisted up."

His grumbling sounds accommodating.

I take a cigarette from the pocket of my backpack, smoke contentedly. Thirty marks saved. That's a book and two records . . .

The man eyes me steadily.

Finally I look over at him.

"Do you drive the same route every day?" I ask, trying to make conversation.

He listens, obviously amused.

"Yeah, I haul books from the headquarters[1] in Leipzig to Berlin. Two times a day."

He still looks at me expectantly.

"And what do you do, if I may ask?" He laughs.

I inhale a few times before I answer. What story should I tell today?

"I go to college."

Already the next question: "What's your field?"

"Education: civics and literature mainly. The only department I could still get into."

The driver's laughing expression slowly disappears.

He starts eyeing me again, scratches the back of his neck.

Then he nods. "So, a teacher . . . civics and literature, aha," he says.

A queer fish, I'm thinking.

"And where do you go to college?"

"In . . . in Leipzig."

"Aaah, in Leipzig?"

"My boyfriend goes to college in Berlin. Now I'm on my way back to class. I cut the one this morning."

The man stares at me incredulously.

I light my next cigarette, offer the package to him. "Have one?" I've never yet met a truck driver who didn't smoke.

"No, but it don't bother me, go right ahead." Even this silly conversation seems to make him thoughtful.

1. The book distribution center in the GDR.

Then he says, emphasizing each syllable: "So, in Leipzig . . . did you grow up there too?"

I'm ready to say yes, then it occurs to me that he could ask which part of the city, the street, etc. So I say: "No, I grew up on the coast, in Kühlungsborn."[2]

He bursts out laughing.

"I see," he says, "so you're from Kühlungsborn."

Then his eyes meet mine. He looks as though he'd like to pull a mask away from my face. "But your accent don't sound like it's from the coast. I'd say it's . . . genuine Saxon with a touch of Berlin. You don't hear that very often. I've only heard it once before." He looks at me challengingly. "That was six months ago, also on the expressway."

What a dope I am, I think. Kühlungsborn, with my dialect. "As a child I was in Saxony for a long time," I tell him. I name a place near my hometown, where I am actually heading. Make up a series of moves adventuresome enough to prompt my own admiration.

The driver looks tense. "And where, if I may ask, do you live in Leipzig?"

"In a student dormitory," I answer. "We're four to a room, it's never quiet enough to study."

"And why do you stay there? You could find a room . . ."

"You try to find one. I put two ads in the paper, hunted up and down the streets every night, nothing."

The man squints over at me.

"Is something wrong?"

"I thought you'd had a room for a long time in Dresden," he answers finally. "A retired lady, I thought, had taken pity on you. . . . And aren't you a nurse?"

I tell him he must be confusing me with somebody.

"You remember last spring?" he asks, speaking slowly and emphatically. "You had on the same jeans with the leather patch

2. A town northwest of Rostock, on the Baltic coast.

on the knee and a red blouse. And you were just as clumsy with your cigarette then. You're getting ashes all over yourself. There's an ashtray on the door, I already told you that once."

He is silent for a bit, then asks: "What are you, really?"

I look over at him. This face, round, somewhat chubby, almost soft . . . doesn't it seem familiar? I feel myself blushing and turn toward the window.

Finally I work up a smile. "Do you think I might have a double?"

The man grins. "I recognized you right away, from your accent. There's not another one like it between Rügen and Fichtelberg.[3] And I don't pick up many hitchhikers. Most of 'em are waiting for somethin' fast. You said before that your father was a bookkeeper, and now he's an officer in Kühlungsborn. What is he, really? And who are you?"

I shove the third cigarette into my mouth, almost light the filter.

"Today's the first time I've ever ridden in such a slow rig," I say. "And you can pay me a visit in Leipzig." Without hesitation I name the street and house number of a student dormitory where a girlfriend of mine lives. "But don't be shocked when you see what a pigpen the area around the dormitory is. Some of them just dump their garbage out the window, don't think it's really their home." I give a long lecture on the dormitory, repeating what my girlfriend has recently told me.

The man is silent.

I'm starting to get uncomfortable. What if he asks for my passport? Should I say that I'd rather get out and wait for something faster?

Outside it's foggy, not a trace of another car. Should I tell the truth?

3. See note 21 of "Feldberg and Back"; her dialect is from the southeastern part of the GDR. Rügen and Fichtelberg are points at the extreme north (island of Rügen) and the extreme south (Fichtelberg Mountain) of the GDR.

Earlier I'd tried that two different times on the expressway. The first time, after making small talk for a while, I explained that I'd studied philosophy in college and was now freelancing, and that I wrote poetry. The driver hadn't said another word for the rest of the trip.

The second time was when a man driving a Dacia[4] had stopped and offered me a ride. He had just given me a line about how you only have to find your "thing" in order to make money, just the dumb ones worked for a living. His "thing" was fashion modeling for television.

I expected the man to ridicule me. Instead he whistled through his teeth. "What am I talkin' about, you got your thing too," he said. "You won't be hitchhikin' much longer. I know a guy in your field. Years ago he wrote a detective mystery about the founding of the GDR just after the war. Now he lives like a king, two houses and an aviary."[5]

After that I lost the desire to tell the truth about myself. In response to the question about what I was, or wanted to be, I started making up stories. A different one for each driver. It was fun and passed the time. Besides, it's easier riding with somebody whose goodwill you enjoy because what you are, or want, falls within his frame of reference.

I'd always had good luck with it.

I reach for my cigarettes again.

"Didn't you say last time you smoked five a day at most?" asks the driver.

I pretend not to hear.

The man looks straight ahead.

"What are you thinking about?" I ask.

"I'm trying to figure out why you tell phony stories. Last spring too. Nurse . . ." He shakes his head.

"And why should I tell phony stories?"

4. A Yugoslavian automobile.
5. A reference to the privileged status enjoyed by writers who curried the favor of political functionaries in the GDR.

"Well, if you were one of these, for example." He makes a movement with his right hand parallel to the floor of the cab.

"One what?"

He repeats the hand movement. "They like to ride in trucks. There's enough room for business."

He delights in my anger.

"I was only joking. I can spot one even before she gets in. I'm allowed to tell stories too, aren't I?"

He takes a box of chocolates out of his worn briefcase, reaches it toward me. "Open it up. They're my cigarettes. Take a couple."

Subdued, I thank him.

The man reaches into the box repeatedly, empties half of it.

"Well, go ahead, why are you being coy?"

I take another chocolate.

"Good?"

I nod. "I like the ones with nuts."

After a while he says, "Maybe you really have a double, a twin sister you don't know anything about. I read somethin' like that once, *Lotty and Her Double.* Ever read it?"

"It's a beautiful children's book by Erich Kästner.[6] Do you read a lot?" I want to get the man thinking about something else.

"Not at home. No time, with family and the garden. But on the road. In back I always have two trailers full of books. When I take a rest, I pull out a book."

"And what do you like to read best?"

He smiles meaningfully. "My favorite is somethin' historical, about the ancient Greeks or Napoleon. There's this new book. By . . . a Frenchman."

"Tarlé?"[7]

"Right! You really keep up with things."

"And books on contemporary subjects?"

6. Erich Kästner (1899–1974), author of *Das Doppelte Lottchen*, 1949.
7. Evgenii Viktorovich Tarlé (1874–1955), a Russian author who wrote a biography of Napoleon.

"Sometimes. You want t'know what you're haulin'. Yeah, these books of today . . . after the first ten pages most of 'em end up back in the trailer."

"Why?" I ask. "You live in the present. And it's interesting to see what other people write about it."

He nods. "But a lot of 'em aren't honest. One time I had a book about a woman, she'd studied architecture, her name was Franziska. That's my wife's name, you see . . ."

"Linkerhand?"[8]

"Yeah, I couldn't put that thing down even though it was so fat. That was somethin'. But a lot of 'em, like I said . . . well, what's the name of this bestseller now?"

I mention the title and author of a novel that's just been praised highly in the press.

"Exactly." In a few sentences he explains why he clapped the book shut after the fiftieth page.

"Just look at the women," he concludes. "None of 'em alive. Like out of a fashion magazine. I wouldn't wanna be married to some dame like that."

"Do you read poetry, too?" I ask.

The man is silent for a long time, looking over at me only now and then.

"If I've loaded on somethin' like that, why not?"

After a while he adds, "Day before yesterday I looked at somethin' by a young woman, she can't be much older'n you." He says my name. "Have you read it?"

"No, I haven't," I stammer. "How did you like it?"

He keeps quiet.

Finally he says, "I don't think she's hitchhiked much before. Did you ever get out of a truck and into a Volvo and have a conversation with the Volvo driver?" He laughs sadly. "We're

8. A reference to the title character of Brigitte Reimann's novel *Franziska Linkerhand*, published in the GDR in 1974.

[133]

such different people when it comes to how we live and think and talk. . . .[9] Aren't you feeling well?"

"Oh, it's nothing . . . we often bring up things like that in the dormitory."

"In the dormitory?" The man laughs.

After a while he asks: "Was that stupid, what I said?"

"No," I answer. "Why?"

He yawns. "Read it through and send her a note. Mention an old trucker recommended it while you were out hitchin' a ride. One of the common folk. By the way," he says and yawns again. "By the way, there's a photograph on the inside of the book jacket. Stick the letter in your own mailbox."

He reaches the chocolates in my direction without looking at me. "Like another one?"

---

9. In the driver's opinion, the poems written by the female hitchhiker reveal both her youth and her inexperience. In writing about the GDR, she has apparently ignored the basic differences that exist between the privileged class, represented by the driver of a Volvo, and the common working man, such as a truck driver.

Translator's Afterword

.

As a writer Gabriele Eckart came of age in East Berlin during the 1970s. Early in the decade it appeared that the East German government was about to relax its hold on the country's cultural life. No taboos, Erich Honecker declared, should restrict the works of writers and artists who themselves were firmly grounded in socialism. In 1972 Heiner Müller's *Macbeth* was staged for the first time. Christa Wolf's novel *Nachdenken über Christa T.* (Reflecting on Christa T.) was permitted a wider circulation than had been the case in 1968. And Ulrich Plenzdorf's fictional narrative *Die neuen Leiden des jungen W.* (The New Sufferings of Young W.), together with his stage adaptation of the same title, inspired the GDR's most spirited literary debates of the early 1970s. Yet another sign of change came from the Seventh GDR Writers' Congress in November of 1973, which marked an official departure from the programmatic Bitterfeld Way. No longer were working-class heroes and didactic political themes the most important issues in East German literature.[1]

In retrospect, however, this thaw in the GDR's political climate was rather slight. Writers who engaged in criticism of the state still did so at their own risk. Rainer Kirsch's satiric comedy "Heinrich Schlaghands Höllenfahrt" (Heinrich Schlaghand's Trip to Hell), for example, was banned from East German theaters

1. Wolfgang Emmerich, *Kleine Literaturgeschichte der DDR: 1945–1988*, 2d ed. rev. (Frankfurt am Main: Luchterhand, 1989), pp.242–48.

shortly after its publication in the monthly theater magazine *Theater der Zeit* in 1973. Two years later Volker Braun's documentary narrative "Unvollendete Geschichte" (Unfinished History) was restricted to the literary journal *Sinn und Form*. A decisive turning point came on 17 November 1976 with the widely publicized expatriation of poet-singer Wolf Biermann. During the remainder of the decade a steady stream of writers, under varying sets of circumstances, were to leave the GDR. In 1976, Thomas Brasch and Bernd Jentzsch; in the following year Sarah Kirsch, Rainer Kunze, and Hans Joachim Schädlich; later in 1977, after imprisonment, Jürgen Fuchs, Christian Kunert, Gerulf Pannach. Between 1978 and 1981 others, such as Jurek Becker, Erich Loest, Günter Kunert, Rolf Schneider, Kurt Bartsch, Klaus Schlesinger, and Karl-Heinz Jakobs took advantage of extended visas in order to live in the West. The decade that began with promises of greater freedom for East Germany's writers and artists ended with the imprisonment of social critic Rudolf Bahro and the exclusion of nine established writers from the GDR Writers' Union.

Despite the heavy-handed interference of cultural and political functionaries, a number of promising developments occurred in GDR literature during the 1970s, especially in literary prose. No longer limited to "socialistic realism," East German writers finally availed themselves of the many techniques associated with modernism. The result was a narrative prose enriched by new dimensions of subjectivity, revitalized language, open forms, parable and myth, highly crafted documentaries, and sophisticated social criticism. A case in point is *Die neuen Leiden des jungen W.* (1973). Plenzdorf's Edgar Wibeau, a young dropout from East German society, narrates his own "story" in his own youthful language without corrective intervention on the part of the author. Like Goethe's Werther, his model, Edgar feels victimized by an authoritarian society's pressures to conform and calls attention to the plight of the isolated individual. Edgar's death, whether self-inflicted or not, serves to implicate his society.[2]

The decade also marked the emergence of key women prose writers in the GDR. Two innovative texts, Sarah Kirsch's *Die Pantherfrau* (1973)[3] and Maxie Wander's *Guten Morgen, du Schöne* (Good Morning, Beautiful, 1977) drew upon tape-recorded interviews in giving individual voices to a cross section of East German women. Bolstered by the documentary claim, both texts effectively undercut the government's stereotyped portrayal of women living under communism. Three novels that addressed the emancipation struggle of women in the GDR and at the same time opened up new themes and narrative modes were published in 1974: Brigitte Reimann's *Franziska Linkerhand*, Gerti Tetzner's *Karen W.*, and Irmtraud Morgner's *Leben und Abenteuer der Trobadora Beatriz* (The Life and Adventures of the Troubadour Beatriz). In their wake appeared numerous collections of prose pieces by and about East German women: Helga Schubert, *Lauter Leben* (Nothing But Life, 1975); Angela Stachowa, *Stunde zwischen Hund und Katz* (The Hour Between Dog and Cat, 1976); Charlotte Worgitzky, *Die Unschuldigen* (The Innocents, 1976); Brigitte Martin, *Der rote Ballon* (The Red Balloon, 1977); Helga Königsdorf, *Meine ungehörigen Träume* (My Improper Dreams, 1978); Monika Helmecke, *Klopfzeichen* (Signals, 1979); Beate Morgenstern, *Jenseits der Allee* (The Other Side of the Street, 1979); Christa Müller, *Vertreibung aus dem Paradies* (Expulsion from Paradise, 1979); and Rosemarie Zeplin, *Schattenriss eines Liebhabers* (A Lover's Silhouette, 1981).[4]

Gabriele Eckart's *Hitchhiking* was first published in 1982. It is not surprising, therefore, that her prose tales reflect several of the

2. Emmerich, pp.245–58.

3. Sarah Kirsch had already won a considerable reputation as a poet by this time. See also *The Panther Woman: Five Tales from the Cassette Recorder*, trans. Marion Faber (Lincoln: Univ. of Nebraska Press, 1989).

4. Emmerich, pp.301–2.

developments that took place in GDR fiction during the previous decade, for example, a preference for first-person narratives together with fictional strategies that lay claim to the authentic; an interest in characters living on the periphery of society, especially single women; a concentration on the GDR commonplace, not as a potential utopia but as an everyday environment. At the same time, *Hitchhiking* bears Eckart's own unique stamp. For the benefit of readers approaching her prose tales for the first time, I wish to draw attention to several of their most distinguishing features. For the sake of convenience, I have grouped them under the following headings: (1) social criticism; (2) narrative perspective, form, and the claim of authenticity; (3) settings and characters; and (4) the ironic dimension.

Social criticism: in a totalitarian society, as Thomas Brasch has observed, readers often turn to literary texts for social "truths" denied them elsewhere. Literature becomes a substitute for journalism.[5] As Eckart's prose tales reveal, timely social criticism is an integral part of her fiction. In *Hitchhiking* we encounter travel restrictions, sexual discrimination, shortages of consumer goods, inadequate public services, blatant political propaganda, and a privileged class of citizens, all taboo subjects in the East German media. In more graphic terms, we are exposed to a government building program insensitive to the needs of an elderly couple ("Philemon and Baucis"), a discrepancy between Marxist theory and practice that leads to boredom and indifference on the part of East German workers ("Construction Site"), and to political indoctrination that stunts human development ("Uncle Benno," "Feldberg and Back"). The sole character who endorses the prevailing system of government is an elderly woman, deathly ill, who lives in pitiful isolation ("Old Woman"). As one West German reviewer stated, "It is difficult to conceive of a greater contrast to the official image of people living under socialism.

5. Brasch quoted by Emmerich, p.289.

[138]

Thus it may be surprising, at first glance, that this book could even be published in East Germany."[6]

Narrative perspective, form, and the claim of authenticity: nine of Eckart's prose tales are narrated in the first-person. This fact, it would seem, helped keep *Hitchhiking* from falling prey to East German censorship. Eckart may use either her own name or a fictitious one, or simply leave the "I" unidentified, but all of her female narrator-participants have certain characteristics in common: they are restless, curious, keenly observant, remarkably honest, and responsive to the needs of others. They demonstrate a capacity to endure hardships and to bring about changes. Despite setbacks and disappointments, their outlooks remain warily positive. In only one instance (in the title story) is the narrator deceitful, and in this case she lies openly, with the full knowledge of the reader. Eventually she is put to shame by an alert truck driver who possesses several of her own virtues, such as a good memory and a keen eye for detail. The reader is thus encouraged to trust this first-person voice, or narrative presence, that in turn offers a counterbalance to the many negative aspects of the GDR.

Adding to the veracity of the tales is Eckart's fondness for concrete particulars, especially in accounting for her settings, such as the cellar of a crumbling apartment building in East Berlin ("The Woodlouse"), the fusty dwelling of the Eberlein sisters ("The Attic"), or the reception hall of a village inn in Vogtland ("Uncle Benno"). She also supplies convincing details of "process" in a tale such as "Construction Site." To lend credibility to this particular narrative, Eckart labels it a documentary, although she is obviously as interested in portraying individual characters and dramatizing conflict as she is in conveying information. Early in her career Eckart herself observed that working on a construction site opened up a new language for her. All of

6. Eckhard Franke, "*Per Anhalter*: Gabriele Eckarts Geschichten aus der DDR," *Main-Echo*, 5 December 1986. The translation is mine.

the tales in *Hitchhiking,* whether literary portrait, documentary, or short story, feature lively dialogue and descriptive prose that is deliberately sparse, direct, and informal. The brief, fragmentary paragraphs suggest immediacy rather than calm detachment; often they reflect the narrator in the act of perceiving. Not surprisingly, Eckart avoids conventional plot formulas and frequently opts for the open ending. When she is at her best, the prose forms she employs complement the restlessness as well as the qualified optimism of her narrators.

Settings and characters: although the settings change frequently in Eckart's tales, as befits the title of the collection, East Berlin figures prominently in the majority of them. We are provided with rare glimpses of everyday life in various parts of the city, from a *Kulturhaus* in Friedrichshain to one of the oldest neighborhoods in the borough of Prenzlauer Berg; from inside one of the GDR's huge construction combines to the street sweepers' night shift on Alexander-Platz. Even in "Uncle Benno" and "The Attic," two tales which are set in Eckart's native region of Vogtland, the narrator is seeing with the eyes of one who now resides in the city. Eckart's depiction of East Berlin may reflect some of her own ambivalent feelings in the 1970s, but in general the city remains a place of promise and discovery. As one of her blue-collar workers says, "Yeah, Berlin. Here ya can try out a few things."

Eckart's tales introduce a wide range of characters, male and female; the elderly, the middle-aged, and the young; from single mothers and students to street sweepers, truck drivers and construction workers. Clearly she has a special interest in those who exist on the edges of East German society. Among her most memorable creations, in addition to her individual narrators, are women who find strength to defy societal norms and seek to live meaningfully on their own terms: Mrs. Olschewski in "The Woodlouse," the mother of Ayane in "Saubersdorf," or even Baerbel in "The Tall Girl." In Eckart's best tales, her characters' interactions elevate them above the narrow confines of their lives. A street sweeper with a drinking problem becomes MAN struggling alone to regain his last traces of dignity; a young female student who shares his shift assignment becomes WOMAN endorsing hope and the human community ("Street Sweepers").

The ironic dimension: Eckart's deceptively simple prose makes it easy to overlook both the ironic and the paradoxical dimensions of her tales. In several instances a character is revealed to be the reverse of what he or she appears to be. In "The Tall Girl," for example, Manfred may have distinguished himself as a lifesaver while in the army, but by the end of the tale we learn how misleading his reputation is. In other instances the ironic dimension is an integral part of Eckart's social criticism. "Philemon and Baucis" invites a comparison between the generosity of Ovid's visiting gods and the indifferent East German government. In "Street Sweepers" the notion of workers' solidarity is innocently expressed by a young intellectual: "Nobody steals here." Yet the street sweepers in the tale have already stolen—in this case a fellow worker's freedom and dignity. Irony also comes into play on rare occasions when Eckart distances herself from her first-person narrator. In "Construction Site," the young woman's private victory hardly warrants the conclusion she draws at the tale's end. And while the narrator in "Hitchhiking," the title story, may be approaching her geographical destination, Eckart implies that she still has a long way to go as a writer, despite her verbal agility and lively imagination.

One of the most engaging problems that I have faced as a translator is rendering Eckart's colorful dialogue, including the Berlin and Saxon dialects, in appropriately informal English. Rather than compensatory dialects, I have resorted to different levels of colloquial English to convey the distinctive spoken language, say, of a young cement worker, an aging widow from the provinces, and a veteran crane operator using the Berlin dialect. At the same time, I have sought to approximate the informal diction of Eckart's narrators, and to preserve the rapid pace of her short, staccato sentences and abrupt paragraphs. For the benefit of those unfamiliar with special abbreviations, places, and terms relating to the GDR, I have included explanatory footnotes.

In the wake of German reunification, it should perhaps be pointed out that *Hitchhiking* was first published in East Germany some seven years before the widespread protest actions that brought down the Berlin Wall. In retrospect, Eckart's social criticism anticipates this unrest, and her reference to the young long-haired minister in East Berlin ("A Week in Berlin") hints at the active role the Protestant church would play. But even more relevant in this context, it seems to me, is her continued insistence on the individual's need to seek out his or her own destiny. With *Hitchhiking* Gabriele Eckart has made a unique contribution to contemporary German literature. In translating her prose tales into English, I hope to help her win the international audience she richly deserves.

Selected Bibliography

•

East Germany

Poesiealbum 80 (Poetry Album 80). Berlin: Neues Leben, 1974. (Poetry)

Tagebuch (Diary). Berlin: Neues Leben, 1979. (Poetry)

Per Anhalter: Geschichten und Erlebnisse (Hitchhiking: Twelve German Tales). Berlin: Neues Leben, 1982. (Fiction)

Sturzacker (Plowed Field). Berlin: Der Morgen, 1985. (Poetry)

Seidelstein (Seidel Stone). Berlin: Der Morgen, 1986. (Fiction)

Frankreich heisst Jeanne: Drei Erzählungen (France To Me is Jeanne: Three Tales). Berlin: Der Morgen, 1990. (Fiction)

West Germany

So sehe ich die Sache: Protokolle aus der DDR (That's How I See It: Recorded Interviews from the GDR). Cologne: Kiepenheuer & Witsch, 1984. (Literary journalism)

Per Anhalter: Geschichten und Erlebnisse aus der DDR (Hitchhiking: Twelve German Tales). Cologne: Kiepenheuer & Witsch, 1986. (Fiction)

Wie mag ich alles, was beginnt (Liking Everything That Begins). Cologne: Kiepenheuer & Witsch, 1987. (Poetry)

Other volumes in the European Women Writers Series include:

Artemisia
By Anna Banti
Translated by Shirley D'Ardia
Caracciolo

*Bitter Healing: German Women
Writers from 1700 to 1830*
An Anthology
Edited by Jeannine Blackwell
and Susanne Zantop

The Book of Promethea
By Hélène Cixous
Translated by Betsy Wing

Maria Zef
By Paola Drigo
Translated by Blossom
Steinberg Kirschenbaum

Woman to Woman
By Marguerite Duras and
Xavière Gauthier
Translated by
Katherine A. Jensen

The Tongue Snatchers
By Claudine Herrmann
Translated by Nancy Kline

Mother Death
By Jeanne Hyvrard
Translated by Laurie Edson

The House of Childhood
By Marie Luise Kaschnitz
Translated by Anni Whissen

*The Panther Woman: Five Tales
from the Cassette Recorder*
By Sarah Kirsch
Translated by Marion Faber

*On Our Own Behalf:
Women's Tales from Catalonia*
Edited by Kathleen McNerney

Absent Love: A Chronicle
By Rosa Montero
Translated by Cristina de la
Torre and Diana Glad

The Delta Function
By Rosa Montero
Translated by Kari A. Easton
and Yolanda Molina Gavilan

Music from a Blue Well
By Torborg Nedreaas
Translated by Bibbi Lee

Nothing Grows by Moonlight
By Torborg Nedreaas
Translated by Bibbi Lee

Why Is There Salt in the Sea?
By Brigitte Schwaiger
Translated by Sieglinde Lug

The Same Sea As Every Summer
By Esther Tusquets
Translated by Margaret
E.W. Jones